THE PERFECT TIDE

THE HAWAIIAN GETAWAY SERIES
BOOK 3

MEGAN REINKING

CONTENTS

Editing by Jenn Lockwood

Proofreading and Internal Formatting by Yours Truly Book Services

Cover Design by IndieSage

For Mom and Dad.

1

QUINN

I sing along to the lyrics of "Don't Stop Believin'" by Journey that's blasting from the speakers connected to the DJ's booth, feeling the beat reverberating deep in my bones. A gust of humid Hawaiian air sweeps across my face and through the low bun of loosely twisted curls that are settled at the base of my neck.

My brother, John, spins me on the dance floor, my head falling back in laughter as he gently tugs on my arm, pulling me close before spinning me out again.

"I love this song!" he shouts as he bobs his head to the beat, smoothing his hands down the front of his cream tux. Dancing around me, he weaves between the other wedding guests that are with us on the overcrowded dance floor. A grin grows wild on my face as I watch the way he happily spins around. John married the love of his life, Mia, a few hours ago in a beach ceremony along the coast of Oahu. It's truly been nothing short of an amazing day celebrating the love they have for each other. I may have my own unpopular opinions about relationships and marriage, but I admit, what they have is truly beautiful.

John's been through a lot of heavy stuff the past several years, most recently struggling with PTSD after serving in the Army, not to mention everything that happened with our parents. It feels really good to see him actually embracing and enjoying life. Both he and Mia are basking in the sweetest just-married, happily-in-love glow. Although, the shots of Casamigos the wedding party had after the ceremony may be adding to that glow, if I'm being honest.

We lip-sync the song lyrics in unison, John holding an invisible microphone to his mouth. As we dance, the daylight continues its gradual fade as the soft light from the surrounding torchlights slowly get brighter.

The wedding reception is being held in an outdoor garden area of a local resort that's right off the beach. A sea of circular tables are spread out across the courtyard next to the dance floor, each one draped in ivory and white linens. Blush-pink and sage-green accents decorate each table while an ethereal-looking tent hovers above, string lights drooping down from each corner. It's absolutely magical.

The song ends, and the piano prelude of a slow song starts playing. I'm grateful for the opportunity to slow down and catch my breath—although I do fully relish the energy that's pulsing through me.

"One more?" John asks, smiling and holding his hand out to me.

"Sure," I say breathlessly with a smile. I wrap my hand in his and bring my other arm around his shoulders, feeling protected and safe, the way you do with your big brother.

"What a day, huh? You look happy, bro," I say, studying his blue eyes and carefree expression. He sways me side to side, softly squeezing my hand, then his mouth curves up into a gentle smile.

"I really am, Quinn," he says sincerely. "Thanks for being a part of this today. Couldn't imagine doing it without you."

"We're a team, remember?" As I speak the phrase that we've said to each other countless times, I start to feel the familiar ache in my chest building. I desperately hope that my smile hides some of the emotions that have been threatening to bubble over all day. I refuse to put a damper on his big day, but it's near impossible to shake the reminder of who's missing.

Of who should be here.

Both of our parents were killed in a car accident on their way home from a dinner event when we were in high school. I was in tenth grade. John was a senior. We were still so young, yet left to struggle with the sudden loss of the two most significant people in our lives.

It's been about seven years, and I've learned how to live with my grief, carrying it with me in the deepest part of my bones like a painful companion that won't ever go away. I tend to keep it tucked deep down, much preferring to live in the present. However, big celebrations and life events like John's wedding today make it sit a little closer to the surface, a constant bleak reminder that I've carried with me all day.

As the song comes to an end, I do what I usually do when I think of my parents—find a distraction. Something that will fill me with good feelings. Happy ones. To balance out the raw, tough ones that consume me when I think of them. That's how I live every day—in a constant search of excitement and adrenaline to counteract the heaviness within me. My life is a continuous see-saw of ups and downs, like the rise and fall of the tide.

"Well," I say, patting his shoulders, then fixing his tie. "Thank you for the dance. I need to use the ladies' room."

"Come find me if 'Livin' on a Prayer' comes on!" he shouts,

and within mere seconds, he's scooped up by Mia's aunt, who's been waiting impatiently in the wings to pounce on the groom. With a laugh, I start weaving through the tables, making my way to the bathroom that's just inside the resort's patio doors.

Once inside, I set my beige clutch on the counter and pull out a tube of lipstick to re-apply. The pale-mauve pigment perfectly complements the blush-pink satin bridesmaid dress I'm wearing. A wisp of my chocolatey-brown hair came loose from dancing, so I tuck it back in with a spare pin that I threw in my purse for this very reason. I'm tightening the back of my earring when the door swings open.

"Quinny!"

Tori, my friend and the sister of John's best man, Matt, comes strolling in, setting her black purse next to mine.

"Ah! You look gorg!" She gives me a quick hug. "These bridesmaid dresses are so pretty. This color with your skin tone. Absolute perfection."

"Thanks, girl. Same to you. I'm loving this navy-blue moment you're having." I wave my hand over her strapless dress that's cut just above her knee.

"Yeah, well, as of last week, I am officially single again. Gotta get back out there. Be on my A-game…you never know, you know?" She smirks.

"Oh, I know," I laugh, "any luck so far?"

"Nope," she sighs, running her fingers through her loose blonde curls. "It's kind of hard to date when you were born and raised on an island. I was hoping a wedding with out-of-towners might have at least a couple of options for me."

"I keep telling you, it's easier if you don't put so much stock in men and who's paying attention to you or not," I say with a shrug of my shoulders. "I'm hardly ever disappointed."

"That's because you could care less about dating," she says pointedly, then sighs. "I think you're onto something, though—that seems way less stressful."

I smile, loop my arm through hers, and we head out of the bathroom. We walk back outside toward the bar nestled at the corner of the dance floor. Tori and I have known each other almost our whole lives, since our brothers are childhood friends, but being that she's a couple years older than me, we never really spent time together until I moved home to Hawaii from Alaska last year.

We have several of the same acquaintances and ended up spending a lot of time together in our friend group. Now, I consider her one of my favorite friends. It's not often I can find people who compliment my spontaneous, free-spirited side, but Tori's right there with me—always up for a new adventure.

"Oh! Can I come over tomorrow? I still want to see the photos you took in Spain!" she asks, her blue eyes sparkling. I just got back from a solo trip I took to Madrid, where I spent three weeks wandering in and out of art museums, strolling through their many parks, and sampling as many tapas as I could. I've always enjoyed traveling, but it's become more of a way of life for me the last several years. If I'm in one place for too long, I start to crave new experiences, new surroundings, new people. I have an insatiable wanderlust that I feel deep in my bones. I just can't get enough.

"Absolutely. But don't come before noon. The day-after-a-wedding hangover is real," I laugh.

"Deal. I'll bring greasy takeout to bring us back to life," she says with a smirk.

As we approach the bar, we see Matt in his tux, leaning with one elbow on top of the bar, the other arm holding his seven-month-old daughter, Noelle.

"Aw, come here, princess. Auntie Tori wants to dance." Tori settles her niece in her arms and ventures onto the dance floor while I order a glass of champagne from the bartender.

"She's adorable," I tell Matt, leaning my back lightly against the bar while I wait for my drink. "Seriously. One of the cutest flower girls I've ever seen."

"Oh, don't let her sweet face fool you. She's got a wicked streak that's ready to come out any minute. It's officially way past her bedtime, so the switch should be flipping anytime now," he muses.

"Where's Paige?" I ask, looking around for his wife.

"She's dancing with Elliot." He points to the other side of the dance floor, where Paige is doing the robot with their adopted seven-year-old son. They look absolutely ridiculous making sharp movements with their arms and necks. I catch the look of complete adoration in Matt's eyes as he watches them.

"You are a lucky man," I tell him, which honestly is meant to be a jab at their dance skills, but there's also a sliver of truth in my words. If I was looking for a serious relationship, I would definitely want to find someone who looks at me the way Matt looks at Paige.

"Don't I know it," he murmurs, taking a sip from his beer, "Anyway, how are you doing? All this lovey-dovey stuff making you nauseated yet?" he teases.

I roll my eyes. "I have no problem being around couples in loving relationships."

"You just don't want to be in one," he says smugly, more of a statement than a question, knowing he's completely hitting the nail on the head.

I sigh, not wanting to get into this particular conversation with him. It's true. I think that most long-term relationships inevitably become boring and mundane, and I don't get why people would want to be with the same person for the rest of their lives. Think of all the exciting people they would miss out on meeting and sharing experiences with. However, that doesn't mean I'm incapable of being happy for those that do choose that path for themselves.

"Life's more fun my way," I say simply with a smile.

"Or Brian's way," he chuckles, pointing toward the dance floor. I follow his gaze and find Brian, another friend and groomsman of my brother's, in the middle of the dance floor, surrounded by a posse of women. He looks like he walked right out of a fashion magazine, with his dark, tanned skin perfectly complementing the cream-colored tuxedo he's wearing. His arm tattoos are slightly visible when his sleeve rises up, and his normally tousled, dark brown, messy surfer hair is styled neatly with gel. I watch as he dances coolly between the women, grabbing one woman's hand to slowly turn her in a spin. His posture is strong, with his shoulders set back and a playful grin on his face as he dances. He carries himself with a quiet confidence—not showy at all. And he does look stupidly handsome. I can't blame the women for vying for his attention.

"Does he know all of them?" I chuckle as another woman joins their group.

"No clue. There must be some radar or something coming out of the top of his head that announces he's the only single groomsman. They've been approaching him all night to dance… he's too nice to say no," he laughs, sipping his drink.

"Poor Brian," I say in amusement. I know he can handle himself, but I definitely don't envy him. Single women can be ruthless—especially at weddings.

"I think that blonde one is already planning out their own wedding in her head," Matt says, referencing the woman in the red dress shimmying up to Brian's side. I choke on my laugh as I narrowly avoid spitting my sip of champagne everywhere.

Oh, I definitely like this game.

"And that brunette in the green dress is mentally mapping out the shortest route to take him up to her hotel room," I chime in. Matt smiles and nods his head, then points a finger at the woman in the black dress toward the outer edge of their circle.

"That one's seriously considering faking a rolled ankle to get some one-on-one attention from him."

We spend the next couple minutes commenting and narrating a pretty impressive play-by-play of what we imagine the rest of Brian's evening will look like. It appears his night could go in many different amusing directions. When the song comes to an end, Brian apologetically mumbles something to his fan base and heads in our direction, leaving several disappointed women in his wake.

2

———————

BRIAN

I loosen my tie and unfasten my top button as I walk briskly off the dance floor. I've been enjoying dancing, but I need a break—these women are relentless. Dodging another group of ladies that are chatting in a huddle next to a table, I look up to see Matt and Quinn smiling in amusement as I approach them at the bar.

"Having fun?" Matt offers me a beer with a grin and a mischievous glimmer in his eye.

"Just need a break," I reply curtly, grabbing it and taking a long pull.

"If you don't want to dance with them, why do you?" Quinn asks pointedly. The bracelet on her wrist glimmers in the light as she raises the glass of champagne to her lips. I zero in on it but then force myself to look the other direction. Quinn's always been gorgeous, but she's absolutely stunning today, and I've had to mentally remind myself to look away several times throughout the day when my eyes have caught on her. The way her chocolatey-brown hair is pulled back accents the plunging neckline of the dress. The way her sun-kissed skin is practically glowing. And the way her brown eyes pop beneath her long, mascara-coated eyelashes.

All of it.

It hasn't gone unnoticed, that's for sure—at least not from me. But I mentally shake it off. Being John's younger sister, Quinn was off-limits to me a long time ago. Same with Matt's sisters. We had an unspoken rule that we were not, under any circumstances, allowed to touch any sisters. John somehow got enough courage to test that rule and slipped Tori the tongue in high school, and Matt cold-cocked him a split second after finding out. We've managed to stick to the no-sisters rule ever since.

I lift my shoulders in a shrug. "I figure it takes courage to ask a guy to dance…don't want to hurt their feelings."

"That's sweet," she says, glancing over at me with a smile.

"I don't mind. It's just dancing—nothing I can't handle," I reply.

"You're a better man than I," Matt chuckles.

"Oh, whatever." Quinn rolls her eyes. "Before Paige, you would have eaten up all that attention. Don't even pretend like you wouldn't have," she laughs.

"She has a point." I chuckle and raise my brows.

"This one's for all the ladies," the DJ announces over the speakers as "Girls Just Wanna Have Fun" starts playing.

"Oh, yes!" A grin spreads across Quinn's face, and she immediately sets her glass down. "Gotta go, boys. See ya!" She practically skips off to join Mia, Tori, and Paige on the dance floor, and I can't help but watch as she goes.

"So, you gonna be next?" Matt inquires, shoving me playfully with his elbow. "Now that John's married, you're the last man standing. Any of these females catch your eye? By the looks of it, you could pretty much have your pick."

"Nah, no one's really standing out." I scan the reception area and the many women I've been dancing with, but sadly, I'm just not into it. Ever since Heather broke up with me a few months ago, I have zero ambition to get back into the dating scene. I just don't have the energy or desire to put much of an effort into it. Besides, according to Heather, I'm way too busy, don't have enough time for a girlfriend, and put everyone else in my life before me and my relationship. Not that she's completely wrong in that assessment.

"You're too picky, dude," Matt says, shaking his head.

My eyes catch on the blonde from earlier. Her red dress is cut dangerously short and hugs her curves in all the right ways. There's no question she's beautiful, but for whatever reason, I'm just not feeling it. Two of her friends are huddled close, giggling with each other, and when her eyes meet mine, she shrugs them off and starts heading in my direction.

"Here we go again," Matt mutters under his breath. I press my elbow into his ribs in an attempt to quiet his commentary.

"Hey. You wanna dance?" the woman asks me coyly, a hint of a blush on her cheeks that highlights her nerves as well as the sad fact that there is no way I'll be saying no.

Dammit. Matt's right.

I am too nice.

I take one last swig of beer, then nod my head, holding my hand out toward the dance floor.

"After you."

I can see the sunlight slowly creeping across the room from behind my closed eyelids early the next morning. Stretching an arm above my head, I gradually force them open, letting the light bring me fully awake. I live in an oceanside bungalow that's settled right off one of Oahu's many sandy beaches. The ocean views are absolutely spectacular and 100% why I chose this place when I was looking at buying two years ago, but I underestimated the early morning sunrise that comes right through my bedroom window and directly onto my face. The upside is I haven't had to worry about oversleeping. The sun always wakes me up before my alarm is set to go off.

The light-brown hardwood floor lets out a groan as I step on it, forcing myself upright and out of bed. With a yawn, I run my fingers through my thick hair, shuffling across the room to the ensuite bathroom. While I wait for the shower to warm up, I pull the toothpaste out of my neatly organized drawer, place the cap back on tightly after using it, and brush my teeth as I mentally run through what needs to be done today.

After I've showered and dressed for the day, I head out of my bedroom and down the hallway toward the small living area that sits directly adjacent to the kitchen. Just past the living and kitchen area are two huge windows on each side of the front door that showcase the pink and orange sky from the sunrise that's cresting on top of the ocean.

"Yo, get up, man," I say to the sleeping body on my couch as I walk past and turn right into the kitchen.

"Ugh," my younger brother, Ethan, groans under the pile of blankets surrounding him. I have no idea when he actually came over or how long he's been asleep. Does he live with me? No. Does he take advantage of the fact that I offered him a spot on my couch anytime Mom's working an overnight shift? Yes. Ethan is seventeen—nine years younger than me—and just starting his senior year of high school.

"Come on, get up," I say again, "We've got an eight-hour charter booked today, and you're supposed to help, remember?"

I own my own deep-sea fishing and excursion company that runs fishing and snorkeling charters throughout the waters of the Pacific Ocean that border the island of Oahu. Ethan is my only employee, helping me out in the afternoons and on weekends when he's not in school. I use the word 'employee' loosely since he has the responsibility of a four-year-old and the ambition to match. As with most seventeen-year-old guys, his focus is on one thing and one thing only.

Girls.

With his phone being a close second. Trying to pull his attention away from his phone and motivate him to do something other than text his friends is a futile waste of my energy most of the time. But at the same time, if I don't, who will? Don't get me wrong, our mom does the best she can. But there's only so much you can do when your time is stretched as thin as hers has almost always been. Our dad left when I was twelve. Ethan was three. He just up and left for work one day and never came back. The note he left for my mom that I found stuffed in the kitchen drawer years later said that he was sick of it. Sick of the life they had. Sick of the fighting. Sick of being tied down.

As a result, my mom was forced to pick up as many nursing shifts at the hospital as she could. She worked tirelessly to provide for me and Ethan, but that was also synonymous with being gone a lot. Ethan spent most of his time in daycare, and the after-school programs at my elementary school ended up becoming my babysitter. When the three of us did happen to be home together, it wasn't hard to see that Mom was exhausted and running on empty. Even though she never directly placed any pressure on me, I innately felt pulled to step up and essentially become the 'man of the house.'

I did as much as I could as a twelve-year-old—helped with the laundry, made jelly sandwiches and snacks for the both of us, and vacuumed almost every day. I even helped change Ethan's dirty diapers before he was potty-trained, which alone should convey how desperate I was to try and help. After a few years of watching helplessly as my mom stressed over bills and food, I begged the local fish market to give me a job processing and packing fish when I was fifteen, and eventually, I worked a second job as a busboy at a restaurant in town. Ninety percent of every single paycheck went to my mom to help with expenses, and I put ten percent into a savings account. When I graduated high school, I put that money together with a loan from the bank and bought a thirty-nine-foot off-shore fishing boat to start my own excursion business.

"Heads up," I say as I toss a mini bottle of orange juice in the direction of where I assume his stomach is. It lands with a small thud, and an arm emerges from under the pile of blankets to grab it.

"What was that for? I was getting up," he grumbles. We're complete opposites, the two of us. Where I'm hard-working, responsible, and dependable, he's scatter-brained, lazy, and unmotivated. The matching brown eyes, dark hair, and ink on our arms are the only things that bear resemblance to each other to hint at the fact that we're related.

"What was going on last night?" I ask, checking my watch for the time as I open the package of English muffins I had laid out on the counter after coming home from the wedding last night in anticipation of breakfast this morning, popping two slices in the toaster.

"Party at Ricky's. Thanks for letting me crash." He takes a long swig of the juice. "So, who we got today on the boat?"

I wrap the freshly peanut-butter-laden English muffins in two napkins, slide one down the countertop for Ethan, and slip my phone into my pocket. I bite into an apple while sliding on my sandals, then grab my neoprene fishing shoes to bring to the boat.

"We've got a group of tourists in town for a wedding. Four guys total. All experienced anglers, so we shouldn't have to do a lot of babysitting."

He nods, pulling a long-sleeved fishing shirt over his head, and slowly shuffles toward the door at a snail's pace. Frustration bubbles inside me, and I push my lips together in an attempt to stop the words that I'm thinking from flying out of my mouth.

"Any day now, dude," I say, not even bothering to hide the annoyance in my voice at this point. "We gotta prep the boat. Think we can pick up the pace a little bit?"

He rolls his eyes, increasing his speed just slightly. I let out a sigh as he passes by, shutting the door behind us.

3
____

QUINN

I hum the tune of "I Gotta Feeling" by Black Eyed Peas as I rub my still sleepy eyes and make my way toward the kitchen in my apartment—or, I should say, Matt's apartment. He lived here by himself for a few years, but when he and Paige got married, they bought a house right down the road to better fit their growing family. He so kindly offered this apartment to me since I was still crashing with John and Mia at the time. Even though this is temporary, it's been very nice to have a place of my own.

When things with Justin, my ex in Alaska, crashed and burned, I was itching to get out of there and desperately needed a fresh start. I came home to Hawaii to visit John until I figured out my next steps, but it turns out I have no idea what my next steps are because it's been more than a year since I've been back, and I still have no clue where I want to settle next. It's almost like there are too many options of places that I'd love to live, and for some reason, I've been super indecisive on narrowing it down. The world is my oyster, and I'm having a hard time choosing where to plant my feet next. Luckily, while I figure it out, I've been able to appease my incessant travel bug with a few trips here and there—my trip to Madrid being the latest.

I power on my espresso machine and decide on a vanilla latte to start my day. As an avid fan of caffeine in all of its forms, my list of favorite coffee drinks is long, and my drink of choice usually depends on my mood that day. Although, lately, I've been leaning toward either a latte or an Americano to start my day. I'm just about to add the freshly frothed milk into the mug when I hear the turn of the door handle.

"Knock knock," Tori says, opening the front door, holding two brown paper bags from a local diner in one hand. She's wearing an oversized gray T-shirt with black leggings, and she's shuffling around on her white Crocs that have a fuzzy liner in them. I stifle a laugh at her choice of footwear. They look absolutely ridiculous, even though I can vouch from experience that they're the most comfortable pair of sandals you could possibly wear.

"I brought hangover food," she mumbles with a miserable smile. "Breakfast sandwiches and hash browns."

"Hi," I chuckle and wave her in, setting my latte to the side, and then get started making another latte for her. "I'm actually doing alright. I feel pretty good today."

"Ugh, seriously? That's super annoying." She laughs softly. "Apparently, I had one too many glasses of champagne." She sinks into one of the chairs at my kitchen table and blows out a slow breath, pressing her fingers to her temple as if the simple act of breathing makes her head hurt.

"Honestly, I think I danced and sweated out any alcohol that was in my system," I admit with a sympathetic smile, bringing both mugs over to sit next to her.

"When do your aunt and uncle head back home?" she asks, slowly unwrapping and taking a bite of one of the sandwiches.

"They left this morning, actually. Had to get back to work."

"California, right?"

"Yup." I've always been close with my aunt and uncle. They became our legal guardians after our parents died. At the time, neither John nor I could stomach the thought of staying in our house after they were gone, so we ultimately decided to move in with them. They ended up moving to California for my uncle's job after I was in college and John had joined the Army. They come back to Oahu occasionally to visit, and I try my best to visit California, but it's not uncommon that long stretches of time pass between seeing them in person. We always soak up any time that we do have together, so I'm sad to see them go.

"Alright, show me these pictures from your trip," she says, grabbing our empty mugs while I gather our garbage. Once I throw it in the trash, I practically skip with excitement ahead of her to the coffee table.

"Seriously, how are you this chipper?" She sounds slightly disgusted, flopping down onto the couch. With a laugh, I grab the photo album off of the coffee table, lowering myself onto the couch, slightly angling myself toward her. Getting situated, I pull my hair up into a topknot and fix the strap of my black tank top that had fallen off my shoulder.

"I still can't believe you went all the way to Madrid by yourself," she says, lifting her brows up in disbelief.

"Honestly, I prefer traveling by myself. I can be on my own timeline and go at my own pace. I don't have to worry about what anyone else wants to do. It's the best way to travel, in my opinion."

"Doesn't it get lonely? I feel like I would miss having someone to share it all with."

"I like being alone," I say with a smile, "Okay, start here," I tell her, opening the album to the first page and sliding it onto her lap. "Tell me your honest thoughts."

I brought my Canon DSLR along on the trip and used it as an

opportunity to dive a bit deeper into the world of photography. Back when I graduated high school, I didn't have much of a plan for where to go for college, but I knew I needed the polar opposite of everything familiar here in Hawaii. I found that in Alaska. Both my guidance counselor and grief therapist encouraged me to try something that might fuel my creative side, so I decided on pursuing an art degree at the University of Alaska Anchorage. I was decent at free-hand drawing, photography, and painting, but none of those felt like a real calling to me at the time. I wasn't passionate about any of them. Not sure what I wanted to ultimately pursue, I ended up finding a job as a floral designer after graduation until I moved back home last year.

I found the camera, that I had purchased second-hand from the school, packed away in a box last month and decided to take it with me to Madrid. I brought it with me everywhere and sort of naturally fell into a rhythm of taking pictures every place I went. It sparked something in me. I'm not sure what, but whatever it was, I felt it strongly enough to force me to pay attention to it and to feel like I'd like to explore photography further.

"Oh my gosh," Tori gasps, zeroing her focus in on the pictures. "This is beautiful." She points to a landscape shot I took in a rose garden—a close-up of a red flower with a sun ray streaming through a thin petal on the upper left corner.

"That one I took at the Parque del Buen Retiro. It's this gorgeous park right in the city. It used to belong to the Spanish monarchy, and it's packed with beautiful monuments, gardens, and fountains," I say. "Ugh, it was one of my favorite places to go. I spent many afternoons at one of their open-air cafes with my camera in hand."

"That sounds like a dream, Quinn. An absolute dream."

"I took this one in the same park." I point to a picture on the next page. This one is a shot of The Monument to King Alfonso

XII in the background with a man and wife in a rowboat on the lake in the forefront of the image. Lush trees and greenery fill the space behind and around the monument.

"It's stunning." She flips through the album, voicing her praise on the different landscape and architectural photographs I took. "I think you should definitely pursue this, Quinn. You have a natural talent for photography."

I stay quiet as I take in her words, letting them sink in.

"I'm serious." She glances at me. "I'm not just saying that because I'm your friend. Is that something you want to do? Pursue photography?"

"I mean, I don't know if it'll eventually turn into anything, but I definitely want to get some more practice. Explore it some more, see how it feels."

"You totally should," she says earnestly as she flips the last page.

"We'll see," I say, taking the closed album from her and laying it on the coffee table. "Anyway, what are you up to the rest of the day?"

"I'm meeting my sisters at the mall in a couple hours. I don't have any house showings or appointments lined up for work, so I'm taking advantage of a quieter day. What about you?"

"Fun. I'm working a shift at Julie's this afternoon." Julie owns a coffee and juice shop in town. Since I haven't been sure how long I plan to stay in Hawaii, I've been reluctant to be locked down with a full-time job. Luckily, I've been able to pick up shifts here and there for Julie. I also help Matt out at his bar a couple nights a week, doing whatever he needs me to do—usually serving or bartending. The money I make from those jobs is enough to pay the ridiculously low rent that Matt charges me and refuses to increase. My parents left an inheritance for John and me after they passed, so I use that money to fill in the rest of the cracks of life and to fund my travels—although I do pride myself on knowing how to travel on a budget, so I don't end up spending a whole lot.

"I'm off tomorrow, though. You want to do something?" I ask.

"Definitely. I have some paperwork to sort through in the morning and an open house tomorrow night, but I'm free in between!" Tori works at a local real estate firm based out of Honolulu. In my opinion, she's one of the best agents on the whole island.

"Okay, I'm gonna go home and sneak in a quick nap," she says, standing up. "I'll call you in the morning, and we'll see what kind of mood we're in."

"Sounds good." I grin, waving as she walks to the door. After the door shuts behind her, I run my fingers over the photo album and let my mind wander, wondering if this just might be worth getting my hopes up for. Will it be the one thing that finally sticks? The thing I'll finally connect with and find purpose in? Some kind of solid direction for my life?

With one last contemplative sigh, I tap the top of the album as I climb off the couch and head to take a shower and officially start my day.

4

BRIAN

"Hey," a familiar voice calls behind me as I'm bent over, rearranging life jackets into the side compartment on my boat. When I turn my head, I'm surprised to see Quinn standing right next to the boat on my dock slip.

"You just get back from a trip?" she asks brightly, pulling her sunglasses up and onto the top of her head, her brown eyes landing on me. She's wearing cut-off jeans and a cropped tan tank top, the lines of her black swimsuit top peeking out by her shoulders.

"Yup." I straighten and twist to face her, walking around the center console to get closer. "Took a husband and wife for a quick fishing trip this morning."

"That sounds fun," she says.

"It was, but they're here on their honeymoon, and I don't think this was the wife's idea of a perfect outing," I laugh as I wipe the sweat from my forehead with the back of my hand.

She smiles back, then her eyes roam around the boat. "Is it just you? Do you take them out by yourself?"

"Yup. My brother usually helps out with the full-day ones. There are usually more bodies on board, so it's nice to have an extra hand with those. But these smaller ones, I just handle myself."

"Cool." She nods casually, looking me straight in the eye. I get sucked into the warmth behind her brown eyes, and neither of us look away for a few moments.

"So, what's up?" I eventually ask curiously, wondering why she's here. It's not like her coming to the marina every day is a normal occurrence. Actually, I don't typically see her at all except for when she's with John, and we're all together as a group. He and Mia left for their honeymoon yesterday, and I just talked to him on the phone earlier, so I'm assuming she's not here because of them.

"I uh…I have a favor to ask," she says sheepishly, her nose crinkling slightly.

"Okay…shoot." I cross my arms loosely over my chest, patiently waiting for her to spit it out.

"So, you know the Makapu'u Point Lighthouse?"

I nod slowly, wondering where she's going with this and what in the world the lighthouse up the coast has to do with anything.

"Well, I'm dying to photograph it, but I would love to capture it from the ocean's viewpoint. I was wondering if you could maybe take me there on your boat sometime?"

"Oh," I say in surprise. Her asking me for a favor, especially one like this, is completely out of character, so it takes me a second to process what she's asking.

"I know it's a lot to ask," she rambles, scratching at her head, "with gas prices, and the time commitment and every—"

"We can go now," I offer with a shrug. I have a hard time saying no in general when people ask for favors, but add the look on her face to the equation, and it makes it near impossible. The slight flush of nerves that crosses her cheeks seems out of place for her. The Quinn I know isn't apprehensive about anything. I don't like that even a small part of her would feel uncomfortable talking to me, so I wanted to make sure I was quick to reassure her.

Her mouth falls open slightly while her eyebrows fly up in surprise. "Really? I mean, it doesn't have to be today."

"No, let's do it," I assure her. "That was my only charter for the day, and everything else can be pushed back, so I have time if you want to go now?"

"Oh my gosh, that would be amazing!" she squeals, lighting up with excitement and clapping her hands together. "Thank you so much, Brian! I'll owe you big time, I promise."

"No worries," I snicker, fully enjoying her enthusiasm.

"My camera's in my car. I'll go get it!" she yells, already running off the dock. "Be right back! Don't go anywhere or change your mind!"

I smile in amusement and shake my head as I check the gas gauge and prep the boat to head out again. This isn't exactly how I planned to spend my afternoon, but I truly don't mind, especially when it involves being out on the ocean again. I could be out there all day if I had to and never get sick of it.

"Okay, I'm ready," she says when she returns, stepping into the boat without even waiting for me to offer her a hand. She slides her sunglasses back onto her face and slings a black camera bag off her shoulder.

"Why don't you slide that under the seat here?" I point underneath the captain's bench that's situated on the center console part of the boat. "Less chance of getting splashed."

"Oh, perfect," she says, going to the far side to slide it under.

I start untying the ropes and pulling the buoys inside the boat. She jumps in to help, untying a rope at the stern. When everything's stowed where it needs to be, I put a bent knee on the cushion of the seat and start to slowly reverse the boat. Quinn slides onto the bench seat next to me. She ties her hair back behind her neck, and when the wind shifts, I can smell a hint of coconut and vanilla.

"Here we go." I push down on the gear to accelerate and get up on plane. She shoots me an unbridled grin as I pick up speed, which makes the corner of my mouth lift up in return. We spend the next twenty minutes cutting through the waves as I take us along the southeastern coastline of Oahu. As we continue on, we pass long stretches of sandy beaches—some splattered with people, others nearly vacant—with lush green vegetation and towering mountains in the backdrop. Eventually, the red roof of the lighthouse sitting on a ridge comes into view. I slow to an idle when we get close enough, and Quinn reaches under the seat for her camera.

"This a good spot?" I ask.

"It's perfect! Thank you." She climbs up to stand on the fishing platform on the bow of the boat and brings the camera up to her eye, angling it toward the lighthouse. Unable to do much else, I stay behind the wheel and watch her as she moves her body to find the best angle. She shuffles to the side a couple of times and then crouches down, resting her elbows on her knees. Then, she moves to the left a few steps, straightening her back to get a slightly higher angle. After several long minutes, she turns to grin at me.

"This is amazing," she says excitedly. I watch as the smile on her face remains unchanged as she looks at the back of her camera.

"So, photography, huh? I didn't know that was something you were into." She's always had an artsy vibe to her, even as a kid, but I don't think I've ever seen her with a camera in her hand.

"Yeah," she says, scrolling through the images on the camera display screen. "I studied it a bit in college but didn't do a whole lot with it. Just picked it up again a little while ago, and I'm really enjoying it. I'm trying to get some more experience with it, and play around with what style and techniques I gravitate toward the most. I want to get some lifestyle shots in, too, but I figured I'd start with more landscape stuff. Hence the lighthouse."

"Cool," I reply, nodding my head in approval.

She lowers her camera, takes a deep breath, and looks around us—taking everything in like she's soaking up every last detail.

"You ever just come out here by yourself? Take your boat out on the ocean and just…go? See what you see?"

I shrug, holding back a laugh.

"Not really." I have an almost visceral response to the idea of doing something that impulsive. I've always been more of a structured, regimented kind of guy, focusing on doing what needs to be done so the next thing on the list can get done. I can't say there's a whole lot of spontaneity in my life—a product of my childhood, I guess.

Now, last-minute favors like this for the people in my life are another story—and happens quite often. I'm just not good at saying no. I have a knee-jerk reaction to say yes when someone asks for help, regardless of what it is they're asking for. But I honestly can't remember the last time I did something spontaneous just for my own enjoyment.

"Oh man, you're missing out. If I owned my own boat—and knew how to operate a boat, for that matter—I would be on it all the time. Imagine all the different things you could do. Where you could go. I mean, I know there are only so many places to go, realistically, but at least you're not stuck on the island."

Her comment makes me smile because it's fitting. Quinn's the kind of spontaneous, thrill-seeking free spirit that I wish I could be more like. She's always had this uninhibited confidence, like she'd be up for anything. I have to say, it looks good on her.

"Why are you smiling?" she asks, eyeing me, her grin growing wider.

I chuckle, scratching at my jaw. "I just think it's awesome that you're always up for finding something adventurous to do."

"Are you making fun of me?" She puts a hand on her hip and tilts her head but keeps the smile on her face.

"No," I laugh. "I admire it. Seriously. Not everyone's like that."

She studies me quietly for a brief second. "Are you?"

I lift my shoulders, staring right back. "Too many other things to do," I say, leaving it at that.

"Did you get what you needed?" I point to her camera. "Anywhere else you want to go?"

"I think I got them. We can head back," she replies, walking back to sit next to me on the seat. I nod and turn the boat back in the direction we came from, accelerating to follow the same route. We're only a few minutes into the ride back when I feel a light tap on my upper arm.

"Can you stop?" Quinn yells over the loud noise of the wind and motor. I immediately slow down, and she pops out of her seat, camera in hand.

"Just one more shot. Sorry!" She points the camera straight ahead and to the right, where the sun is streaming directly off of a cliff in the distance. She leans her whole body into getting the perfect angle for the shot, and when she stands upright to check the image, the widest smile spreads on her face.

"Okay, I'm done, I promise," she says with a laugh.

"No worries," I tell her sincerely. I didn't mind a single second of being her chauffeur this afternoon. I shift into gear but go at a slower pace to take our time getting back. Some days the heat is so scorching hot that being outside borders on being uncomfortable, but today is a decent enough day. It's easy to want to go slow and enjoy it. Eventually, we make it to the dock, and she grabs the rope while I grab a post to steady the boat.

"I can't thank you enough, Brian. Honestly, this was amazing," she says, handing me the rope so I can tie us up. Then, she carefully zips her camera back into the case.

"Of course. Anytime," I say before a thought comes to me. "Hey, actually, I have an idea."

"What's that?" she asks.

"Well, you said you wanted to get some lifestyle shots, right? I have a fishing charter booked for tomorrow morning with a family. If it's alright with them, of course, I bet they would love to have some keepsake photos of the trip from an up-and-coming photographer."

I bite back a grin at the way her eyes light up in excitement.

"Oh my gosh, seriously?"

"Yeah. Tourists always like souvenirs like that, especially families. It would probably improve their experience as a whole, so it would be a win for me, too."

"That would be amazing, actually. I would love that," she says, not holding back at all with her giddiness.

"Great. I'll check with them and let you know for sure."

"Okay, awesome. Can I help with anything else as far as shutting the boat down?" she asks, looking around for anything else that needs to be done.

"Nah, I'm good. I'll text you about tomorrow."

"Okay!" She grabs a post and hoists herself out of the boat and onto the dock.

"See ya." She smiles, and I can't stop my eyes from watching her walk away.

5

———————

QUINN

"Are you having the best time on your honeymoon?" I ask John and Mia through the speaker on my phone. I'm sitting in my car in the parking lot of the marina, finishing our chat before I go meet up with Brian.

"Quinn, you would love it here," Mia says, her voice slightly muffled then getting louder as if she took the phone right out of John's hands. "It's absolutely stunning."

They went to Banff National Park—Lake Louise, specifically —in the Canadian Rockies, where they'll stay for the next week before spending the last week of their honeymoon split between Minnesota to visit her family and then California with our aunt and uncle.

"I convinced John to hike The Little Beehive Trail with me today. I'm proud to say he kept up with me the entire three hours," she laughs. "I think all of the hiking I drag him to at home has finally paid off." I smile when I hear John grumbling in the background.

"Anyway, what are you up to?" Mia asks me.

"I'm just sitting in my car at the marina, about to meet up with Brian to take pictures of his fishing charter this morning. I'm really looking forward to it, but I'm a little nervous."

"I bet they'll turn out great," Mia says excitedly. I mentioned my growing interest in photography to them before they left for their honeymoon, and they were nothing but super encouraging. Mia even gave me the contact information for her wedding photographer when I wanted to ask her a question about a specific editing software.

"Tell Brian I say hi and thanks again," John calls in the background. "He stopped by the house yesterday to bring our mail in and drop some chemicals in the pool for us."

His comment reminds me that Brian's one of my brother's best friends, and I probably shouldn't have noticed all of the little things that I did yesterday on the boat. The things that were nearly impossible to get out of my head for the rest of the day. Like the way his dark-brown hair fell messily out of his hat when he took it off to run his hands through it. The way the dimple on his cheek added a soft juxtaposition to the strong line of his jaw and deepened when he smirked. The way his eyes followed every move I made when I was trying to get the perfect shot. The way that gave me the tiniest hint of butterflies. I'm not sure why I've never noticed these things before, but I know I probably shouldn't be noticing them at all.

He's Brian.

My brother's friend.

The guy who's always been a loyal friend to John and is in many of my childhood memories—as far back as I can remember. It's not that he was invisible to me before, but being alone with him yesterday must have opened my eyes in a new way.

"Will do. I'm actually gonna head out. But you guys have the best time! I can't wait to hear all about it."

After saying our goodbyes, I hang up the phone and swing the camera case strap over my shoulder as I hop out of my car. I see Brian as soon as I start stepping down the wooden stairs that lead to the docks. He's wearing a white long-sleeve fishing shirt and black athletic shorts, bent over, rattling something on one of the compartments on the deck of the boat.

"Hey," I call out as I get closer.

He looks up, and the way he smiles has me trying to remember if he smiles at everybody like that. Like he's glad it's me and not anyone else in the whole world. Surely I'm reading it wrong, but it does something inexplicable to my stomach. I can't say I mind it, whatever it is.

"Hey," he responds, offering a hand to help me climb in the boat. I grab it and squeeze slightly as I jump inside with a grin.

"Photographer at your service, Captain."

He chuckles, then points to the bench seat where I sat next to him yesterday. "You can keep your stuff under the seat again if you want."

I slide the camera on top of the seat for now and look over just in time to see a family of four walking our way—a man and woman that look to be in their late thirties, a boy about ten, and a girl that looks to be about seven.

"Anderson family?" Brian asks as they turn down our dock slip.

"Yes! You must be Brian." The man returns Brian's handshake with a nod of his head.

"You got it. Are you guys ready for a fun fishing trip?" Brian asks, giving each of the kids a high-five.

"Are we gonna trap a shark?" the little girl asks with hopeful eyes.

A husky laugh bursts out of Brian, and I smile at the

adorableness of both the girl and the laugh. The boy rolls his eyes in obvious annoyance at his sister.

"We'll just have to see, huh?" Brian answers. "Come on in." He offers a hand to help each of them inside the boat, then gestures toward me. "This is Quinn, the photographer I was telling you about. She'll be taking some pictures while we fish today."

"Nice to meet you, Quinn," the woman says kindly. "I'm Katie. This is my husband, Mitch, and our son, Brody, and daughter, Lucy."

"So nice to meet you guys. Thanks for letting me tag along. I'll try and stay out of your way, so don't mind me. I'll just work around you guys to hopefully get some fun shots."

"Great, thank you so much. It'll be so nice to have photos of this." She smiles excitedly.

"Alright, so just to go over the contract before we head out— you booked a two-hour in-shore fishing trip where we'll stay just a couple miles away from shore," Brian says, flipping through the paper copy of their agreement.

"Yes, sir," Mitch says. "Figured that would be the best option with these kiddos."

"Right on, it'll be great. We should be able to at least catch some snapper and goatfish," Brian says and then proceeds to do a tutorial on the boat and some safety measures.

"Alright, let's head out," he says when the kids have their life jackets tightened, and the family is seated at the back of the boat. Just like yesterday, I help Brian untie the ropes from the dock, and he takes us out of the marina.

We start heading south, the opposite direction he took me in yesterday, and I take in the beautiful coastline of Oahu as we go. We're far enough out to not bother any surfers or kayakers, but close enough to still have a good view of the long stretches of sandy beaches and the colorful tiki huts and food trucks set farther off the shoreline, tucked under canopies of palm trees. He veers left, farther out another half a mile or so, then he slows the boat to an idle.

"Let's try here," Brian says. Lucy claps her hands together in excitement while I grab my camera out of the case. I step off to the side and let them get comfortable with each other while I take a couple practice shots of the coastline, adjusting the aperture and shutter speed until the settings are perfect.

"Here, let's put this squid on the hook and see what we can catch." Brian crouches next to Brody and shows him how to do it carefully. I come up behind them to get an aerial shot of them hunched together.

"Will that catch a shark?" Lucy asks, which makes us all laugh.

The next hour and a half flies by. I become fully immersed in finding creative angles and capturing this sweet family's interactions. The adults put all of the focus on the kids' experience, so there were plenty of opportunities for some good family shots. I got a couple with the dad standing behind the son, reeling in a fish together, a mother-daughter shot of them relaxing on the bench seat when they took a water break, and several of Brian interacting seamlessly with all of them. I have to admit, I'm impressed after watching him on this trip. He definitely knows his craft. Whether it's rattling off some stats about the different kinds of fish in these waters or explaining the gear, it's cute to watch him interact with clients—especially the kids. Something about a muscly, tanned guy with tattoos being sweet with kids makes my insides happy. Eventually, Brian secures the lines and gets the boat ready to head back to shore.

"Well, Lucy, sorry we didn't catch any sharks, but we got quite a few snappers, didn't we?" Brian says as we pull into the marina. He maneuvers the boat effortlessly into the dock slip.

"That's alright. Maybe next time," she says dismissively. "I'm just glad there were snacks." Brian laughs in response as he starts tying up the boat.

After collecting info and an email address to send the photos to, we say our goodbyes, and Brian and I start cleaning up the boat. They chose not to keep any of the fish they caught, so he doesn't need to filet anything, which shortens the end-of-charter checklist. I grab the kids' life jackets, store them back where they belong, and then pick up a few snack wrappers left on the seats.

"That was so adorable," I tell Brian as I take a break to scan through the images on my camera. "You were so sweet with them."

"You sound surprised," he laughs, wiping down the inside of the boat with a towel.

"Oh, look at this one!" I hold the camera out to show him one of the images, and he stops mid-stroke. He slides his sunglasses off, eyes focused on the camera. A sunscreen-laced, woodsy scent invades my personal space as he leans closer to my side, his arm lightly grazing mine.

"I like that one," his deep voice says softly before resuming his task.

"Thanks. Gosh, this was so much fun. And I gotta say, I'm impressed. You're really good at what you do," I tell him sincerely. "I know you've been fishing since you were a kid—I remember you and John going all the time—but it's fun to see you in action. You're like a legit, professional fisherman."

He laughs, scratching at his forearm. "I hope so. Otherwise, I don't know what the hell I'm doing with my life."

"You know what I mean. It's fun to see you in your element." I put the camera away and grab the leftover water bottles from the drink holders.

"Yeah, it's definitely something I've always enjoyed. Actually, your dad was the first one to ever take me fishing— been hooked ever since."

My chest instantly feels like it is filled with cement. The air gets caught in my airway, the way it always does when someone brings up my parents unexpectedly. It's nothing new, and I've come to expect the automatic physical response. It just usually takes a minute or two to let it pass. I let the dread sit heavy in my stomach for a moment, and then I do what I always do when my grief surfaces unexpectedly.

Deflect.

"Hey, John says thanks for swinging by their house yesterday." I force my voice up an octave higher than it wants to come out. I can feel his dark eyes studying me for an extra beat, and I feel exposed in a way I'm not used to. Heat flushes across my cheeks. I can usually shift out of the heaviness faster than this, but it's lingering for some reason.

"No problem," he says quietly.

"Alright," I say with forced enthusiasm, "if you don't need any more help, I'm gonna take off. I want to get some editing done before I work a shift at the coffee shop tonight."

"I'm good…" He opens his mouth to say something else, but I'm already on the dock.

"Thanks again for today, Brian. I really do appreciate it." I flash him my best smile and turn to walk back to my car.

6

BRIAN

I watch her hurry off the dock like it has suddenly caught on fire. I blow out a ragged breath, regret consuming me. I shouldn't have brought up her dad out of the blue like that. Honestly, I don't think I've ever had a direct conversation with Quinn about her parents' death, so I shouldn't have just naively assumed that she would be comfortable with me just blurting it out like that.

Not that John is an open book of emotions, but we've had at least a few heart-to-hearts about it over the years. John will even be the one to casually bring them up in conversation now. I guess I'm used to that level of comfort talking about them.

But, wow, do I feel like the world's biggest jerk because clearly, she shut down the second the words flew out of my mouth. Not that I blame her. As brutal as it was for me when my dad walked out on us, I know it was a much deeper level of grief that they felt to unexpectedly lose two parents at the same time like they did.

The car accident sent shock waves through our community. The whole island was affected by their deaths, including me. David and Leilani Byrd had cultivated a home life that I was desperately envious of as a kid, and I always loved being at John's house. They were the strong, unified parental front that I was missing at home. My own grief was poignant enough after they died, and having witnessed both John's and Quinn's devastation after it happened, I can totally understand Quinn still not wanting to talk about it so many years later.

The chime of my cell phone brings me out of my thoughts. I fish it out of my pocket to see *Mom* displayed on the screen.

"Hey, Mom." I push the speaker option on my phone and set it on the bench seat, so I can use both hands to finish cleaning the boat.

"Hi, Brian. How are you, sweetie?" Her warm voice is almost completely drowned out by the sound of waves gently crashing onto the cement breakwall in the harbor. I brush one hand on the side of my shorts to dry it off, then I turn the volume up as high as it'll go.

"Just got done with a charter. What's up? Is the air conditioning back on today?"

"Actually, that's why I'm calling. Whatever you did yesterday did seem to work. It seems to be cooling fine, but it's making a high-pitched noise that's freaking me out," she says with a nervous chuckle.

"What kind of noise?" I take her off speaker and bring the phone to my ear.

There's muffling and a screech, which tells me that she placed the phone directly on the air conditioning unit. A slight humming sound is barely loud enough to hear over the shuffling of her phone.

"Mom… Mom," I repeat when she doesn't answer. There's more muffled humming, and I can hear the hint of a low shriek hidden behind it.

"Mom," I say louder, sitting down on the edge of the boat, leaning forward to rest my forearms on my legs.

"Hear that?" she asks, finally coming back to her phone after several seconds of nothing but jumbled noise.

"It's too hard to tell over the phone. Why don't I swing by quick?"

"Are you sure? I mean, that would be wonderful, but no pressure, of course." There's always a hint of guilt in her requests, but she and I both know that I'll do anything she asks me to. I'm the only one who will.

"Sure thing. Be there in twenty." I wrap things up at the dock and walk to my truck.

When I pull into my mom's driveway twenty minutes later, I slide my phone into my pocket and head inside. My mom's and Ethan's voices lead me to the kitchen that's directly up the stairs. Both of their heads swing my direction when I come into view from the doorway.

"Hi, sweetie," Mom says, immediately wrapping me in a hug, then leaning back against the counter. "I was just trying to get Ethan to tell me about the kids in his homeroom this year, but of course, he's not giving me anything."

Ethan rolls his eyes, shoving his sandwich in his mouth. "Same kids as last year, Ma," he mutters. "Same friends I've had since I was five."

"Well, you never know," she says, exasperation clear in her voice, along with a twinge of hurt. "Just trying to make conversation." I know Ethan loves our mom, but the way he shows it gets lost in translation most of the time. When our dad left, I was old enough to understand the situation and understand why Mom had to be gone all the time at work, but Ethan was too young. He just grew up knowing that his dad left, and his mom was hardly ever around. She tried to make up for it in the time that she did have with us, but I'm not sure if it was ever enough.

Sometimes I wonder what life would have been like if

things hadn't turned out the way they did. If we had grown up with more than just one inconsistent parent. If I didn't have to step up and be an adult way before I should have. Maybe I wouldn't have had as much weight on my shoulders all these years, and Ethan would be less of a lazy grouch all the time. My mom's not much of a disciplinarian, either. I think her guilt from not being around makes it hard for her to feel authoritative enough to lay down the law with him. She thinks she doesn't have the right to tell him what to do, which is a shame because that's exactly what that kid needs—even I can see that.

"Parent-teacher conferences are coming up soon. Is there anything you want me to talk to your teacher about?" Mom asks, trying again.

"Nope," is his only response. She nods, finally accepting defeat from attempting to get him to engage in some kind of conversation.

"Okay," she says, shifting her focus to me. "How's your business going, sweetie?"

"Great," I reply, taking a Gatorade out of the fridge. "Staying busy. My calendar's staying consistently full, so that's good."

"Well, you are the best fisherman on the whole entire island, so that's no surprise to me." She smiles. "Any new developments as far as expanding? Buying another boat?"

"Not yet." I shake my head, leaving it at that. It's common knowledge that my goal is to buy another boat at some point, but she doesn't know that my plan for this second boat has been for Ethan to run it after he graduates. He doesn't have any interest whatsoever in college and hasn't even shown any ambition toward having a job outside of the work he does for me, so I'm just anticipating that he'll keep working for me. I figure maybe if there's a boat ready and waiting for him to captain, it might spark a little motivation in him. Maybe that's naive of me, but I can't help but try. I haven't had a conversation about it with him yet. That'll happen after I figure out how I'm going to pay for another boat.

There's an annual big-game fishing tournament that's happening here in a couple months that I'm looking at entering. It's a points-based tournament specifically for ahi or blue marlin that the Hawaii Big Game Fishing Club puts on every year. Fishermen travel here from around the world to compete, and the stakes are high. The payout can be upwards of $100,000. I've done it in the past, and the appeal of the cash prize is strong—not to mention the rush I get from competing at something I know I'm good at. Something I love doing.

"Well, I'm proud of you." She smiles at me, her tired eyes creasing at the edges.

"Thanks." I shrug it off, tapping my hand on the counter. "Alright, show me this noise your air conditioner's making."

We start to make our way down the stairs, but I turn back to Ethan before I get to the top step. "Why don't you come watch? I can walk you through how to fix this thing. Then, you'd be able to fix it yourself next time."

"Nah." He pushes his chair back and slides his phone off the counter and into his pocket. "Gotta meet up with Corey. Good luck, though," he mumbles before disappearing out the sliding deck door.

I shake my head and follow my mom down the stairs to the mechanical room in the basement. The low-pitched shrieking noise is audible before I'm even to the bottom step. Grabbing the toolbox off the shelf along the wall on my way, I start inspecting the unit.

"So, you workin' tonight?" I ask, making conversation while I crouch down to look at all angles.

"Yes, another overnight shift tonight. Hoping it's not too crazy," she says. For whatever reason, the ER has been overflowing with people lately. I don't know what it is. But I'll try and get a quick nap in first, then make some soup to leave in the fridge for Ethan before I leave."

I nod, focusing on dismantling the side of the unit. "You really need to just bite the bullet and get a brand-new unit, Mom," I tell her, which elicits a sigh from her.

"I know I do. Maybe with my end-of-the-year bonus money."

"That's months away, Mom. This might not make it that long. There's only so much I can do."

"Well, hopefully, we can keep it kicking until then."

It's not that she can't afford to buy it. She definitely can. Her savings account has grown over the years, especially after I moved out, and she had one less kid to support. It's her mindset that hasn't changed. It's hard for her to wrap her head around spending money when it was so tight for so many years. I can't say I blame her.

I manage to get the noise to stop and the cool air flowing for now, so I put it back together and put the tools back in the box.

"Thank you, sweetie," she says to me when we make it back upstairs to the door. I throw an arm around her and kiss her forehead.

"Anytime. Good luck at your shift." I smile and head out the door, so she can take a nap.

7

____

QUINN

"Come here, keiki (child)," my mother says to me as I climb up into her lap with a book. I'm not much older than six years old. John is playing with his airplanes on the rug in front of us. We're settled in the living room, where we often gather before Dad gets home from work.

Dad opens the door and kicks his shoes off before entering. John and I jump into his arms, and he tickles us both until I'm overcome with laughter, gasping for a breath. I watch as he then crosses the room to Mom and gives her a kiss on her cheek in greeting, one of the many customs my father adopted when he married my mom, who is native Hawaiian.

"Aloha, Leilani."

"Aloha, David."

I watch as they gaze at each other lovingly for a moment, then he sets his keys on the coffee table and lowers himself to the ground to pick up an airplane next to John. I climb back into

Mom's lap and press my back into her as far as I can, relishing in the warmth and comfort I feel as her arms fold around me tightly. She opens the book and starts to read, her breath softly tickling my ear with every word.

I wake with a start, the low hum of the ceiling fan above me the only sound I can hear—that and my shallow breaths. The hollow ache in my chest pales in comparison to the utter emptiness I feel. And the stark reminder that I'm alone. So devastatingly alone. I turn onto my side, wrap the blanket tighter around me and push my face into the pillow, desperately trying to get back to the comfort of my dream that was just within reach. Wishing like hell I knew how to get back there, because that's where my mom and dad are.

In my dreams.

I don't have dreams about them every night, just every so often, but truthfully, I wish I never did. As much as I so desperately cling to the memories and the love that I feel while I'm in the dream, the reality that hits me when I wake up is far too jarring and painful. I have to deal with the reality that they're gone all over again, every single time, like a recurrent reminder of the most painful part of my life. It's an immediate kick to the stomach when I open my eyes. It's exhausting, to say the least.

I so desperately wish I was one of those people who don't remember their dreams. The people who, when they wake up, have no recollection of the world they were just subconsciously in. But that's not me. I remember every single detail, every single feeling that consumed me while in it. Which is unfortunate, because my dream and the mood it puts me in usually stick with me long after I wake. Feeling ready to push the memory back down, I rub my eyes with the backs of my hands.

Any amount of time that I spend thinking about my parents gives me an urge to acknowledge and honor them in some way. To somehow validate how much they still mean to me. So, when

I get lost in my memories, I always say goodbye to them in the same way. By whispering the words my mom would always whisper to me when she tucked me in at night.

"aloha au iā 'oe mau loa.

I love you forever."

Squeezing my eyes shut, I blow out a slow breath and push the blanket off. Time to find a distraction to get me out of this funk. I sit on the side of my bed and unplug my phone from the charger on the nightstand. I go to my Favorites list and call Tori, who picks up after two rings.

"Hey, girl!" she says in a perky voice.

"Hey," I reply, my voice still groggy from sleep and the emotions I'm trying to steer away from. "You want to get together today? I don't work a shift at Matt's until later tonight, and I'm itching to go do something."

"Ugh, I wish, but I can't. I'm holding an open house for one of my clients today, and then I'll be taking some other clients to show them houses this evening. Apparently, everyone decided that this week is a great time to sell or buy," she says with a laugh.

"Hey, that's a good thing, right?" I say. "That's great, actually."

"Yeah, I suppose. The next two days are pretty busy, but I should have some time after that. I'll keep you posted. Maybe we could go paddle boarding."

"Yes, that sounds great! Go kick some real-estate butt," I tell her before hanging up, wanting to be encouraging even though I am disappointed that she can't meet up.

I stare at my phone for a few minutes, trying to think of somewhere outside of my apartment to go. If Tori's unavailable, the next in line is usually John and Mia, but they're still not back yet. After several minutes, I get dressed and grab my keys, knowing exactly where I want to go—not bothering to second-guess or ask myself why.

My feet crunch on the sandy path that winds along the side of Brian's bungalow, coming to a stop at the porch steps that lead up to the front door. The porch swing in front of the window on the left catches my eye as it ever so slightly sways with the sea breeze. The white exterior of the house is framed by a light-brown trim, with bright-green bushes tucked close on each side and a huge palm tree hovering over the top of it. Underneath it, on the right side of the cottage, I can see the outer wall of the outdoor shower that's connected to the house with a surfboard leaning against it.

Farther right is a hammock fastened between two trees, angled toward the ocean behind me, with a palm tree and a row of bushes lined next to it. Sand from the beach runs right underneath his porch, spilling onto the sidewalk and walkway to the right of the house. I've only been here a couple of times with John, but it's just hitting me now how adorable his house and property really are. It's a quintessential Hawaiian bungalow that gives off major tropical vibes.

With the sound of waves crashing behind me, I climb up the steps and knock on the door, anticipation buzzing under my skin, hoping that he'll be around. When the turn of the door handle creaks, relief surges through me. Sure, I could have checked with one of my other friends to hang out or gone and done something on my own, but the truth is, I've really enjoyed spending the last couple days with Brian. I feel comfortable around him, and he has a quiet, calming way about him that I'm drawn to. I could really use his energy today.

"Quinn?" Surprise and confusion flash across Brian's face as he pulls open the door, but I get caught on one other tiny flash of something in his eyes—anticipation. His arm muscles flex under his white T-shirt as he shifts to hold the door open with one hand, the other hand sliding into the pocket of his black swim trunks.

"Hi," I say, doing my best to sound upbeat and plaster a smile on my face. "Sorry to stop by unannounced, but, um…I was wondering if you were busy right now?" Confusion deepens on his face, and he looks baffled by my question.

"Uh, not really. I was just about to go through some work paperwork. Why, what's up?" His brows furrow together as his deep-brown eyes stare intensely back at me, so piercing that I wonder if they can see the mess that's hiding behind mine.

"Do you want to go on an adventure with me?" I ask in the sweetest voice I can muster and pair it with pleading eyes, not saying out loud how much I just need to focus my mind on something else right now—anything else. "I don't have anything to do today, and I'm dying to just go somewhere, or do something, or explore." I shrug. "Just wanted to see if you want to come with me?"

The side of his mouth slowly curves up in a smirk. "Me? What, was everybody else busy? Am I your last resort?" He chuckles, crossing his arms over his chest smugly.

"No…okay, maybe. I did ask Tori first, but you were my second thought, I swear," I say, teasingly poking him in the shoulder. "Besides, you could probably use a break, right? So, really, I'd be doing you a favor."

"Is that right?" he asks in amusement.

"Yes. Take a break from work and come have some fun with me?" I ask, trying to not portray the desperation I feel to be on the move today, to keep my feet moving.

"I dunno, Quinn. It's not that I don't want to. I just have a lot of things I should be working on. My days without charters get filled up fast." He scratches the back of his neck, and the struggle of this decision is written all over his face. I wonder how often he lets his guard down and does something unplanned like this. I think a little spontaneity in his life might be a good thing, but of course, I won't push too hard if he's too resistant.

"Please?" I ask one last time, searching his eyes patiently.

He blows out a breath, raking his hand through his messy hair. He looks hesitant, but eventually, a smile emerges as he brings his eyes back to mine.

"What did you have in mind?"

I don't even bother to hide my grin, excitement rushing through me. I'm so grateful to have found a distraction, it doesn't even matter what we end up doing.

"I haven't thought that far yet," I admit.

He seems to think it over for a minute, running his hand along his jaw, and I start to feel silly for coming over here without a plan. But then he shuts the door behind him and takes a step forward, which has me moving back before he runs right into me. He walks past me, down the porch steps, and then glances back at me.

"Did you bring your suit?"

8

———————

BRIAN

"Are you sure you want to get schooled out there today?" Quinn asks playfully as we wax our surfboards on the beach right in front of my house. "You know I'm an amazing surfer, right?"

"I know you can hold your own," I agree with a laugh. She seems pleased with that answer and resumes waxing her board. The wind whips across my face, and I look out at the ocean, where the swells are larger than they typically are on an average day. I'm confident that Quinn's a strong surfer, otherwise, I would think twice about heading out there today.

"I seem to remember being the first one up on the board when we first took lessons. Do you remember that?" she asks with a laugh, using the back of her hand to brush away a stray hair that fell out of her ponytail.

When we were ten years old, John, Matt and I finally convinced our parents to let us get professional surf lessons after begging relentlessly for a couple years. Admittedly, we all thought it was pretty annoying when they insisted that Quinn tag along, but the joke was on us because she was a natural from day one. She easily became a better surfer than the three of us combined, and I'd say she probably still is.

"I do remember that," I say, waxing the last corner of my board. "We surfed a lot together those early years, didn't we? Except John put his foot down and wouldn't let you come if the swells were too big—no matter how experienced you were." I laugh at how ridiculous that was. Quinn could out-surf him any day of the week. But it was typical John—he has always been an overprotective big brother.

When I finally gave in and let Quinn convince me to abandon my to-do list and join her today, surfing came to my mind right away. I genuinely love to surf. In the rare instance that I have free time, I'm either surfing or hanging with the guys —that's about it. It's one of the few things that I actually do for myself, and it serves as a great stress reliever for me. When I'm surfing, I can let go of the demands of life and my responsibilities. It's just me, my surfboard, and the ocean. Everything else just disappears. No to-do list, no work obligations, and no doing favors for others. I've been wanting to get back out there, so I was glad when Quinn said she was up for it.

"Yeah, John's a pain in the butt sometimes." She stands and pulls her blue tank top over her head, revealing a black bikini top. I force my eyes down when she shimmies off her shorts, but I'm hyper-aware of her out of the corner of my eye. I remind myself—like I have frequently over the past several days—that she's John's little sister.

I wonder what he would think about us spending time together. We hang out as a group all the time, but it's never just her and me. This is all new. But I can't help but be drawn to her more in the last few days than I ever have been before. I'm not sure if it's because John's gone, so it's easier to notice her more, or if it's that I'm realizing that she makes me feel lighter in some way. I can't put my finger on it, but she keeps popping up in my mind. Regardless, it's all harmless. It's not like I'm making a move on her. I know better than that—no matter how good she looks in that swimsuit. And damn, does she look gorgeous.

"Alright." She lifts her longboard, tucks it under one arm, and walks backward toward the water.

"Let's do this!" she says excitedly with a smile, spreading her free arm wide before breaking into a jog toward the water. I quickly grab my board and follow her with a grin of my own. Her enthusiasm is almost palpable. I feel like I'm being sucked right into it—like the inevitable force of a magnet.

Her feet hit the water seconds before mine, and I follow slightly behind her on her left as we paddle out. Straddling my board, I watch as Quinn squares her board with the next wave, shifts forward when the wave just starts to lift the trunk of the board, and pops up to her feet as she effortlessly rides the wave. I follow with the next wave, and we spend the next forty minutes taking turns alternating waves, fully caught up in the intricate process of surfing, until we eventually trudge out of the water, lungs burning and legs throbbing.

I collapse next to her on the sand and unfasten the leash from my ankle, adrenaline buzzing through me. Not only is surfing a great stress reliever, but the high I get from it is unlike anything else. The way I can slip out of reality for a little while and focus only on my technique and the wave is like my own escape. It's stupid that I don't do it more often, given I can literally see my house from here.

"That was fun," I say between gasping breaths. "Thanks for dragging me out of the house. That was much needed."

Quinn pulls her long, wet hair over one shoulder, then wraps her arms around her bent knees. She turns her head until her brown eyes lock with mine. It's then that I notice the tiny birthmark that sits just below her left eyebrow. It's small but definitely noticeable. I wonder how I've never noticed it before.

"When's the last time you surfed?" She peers at me, out of breath herself. I shrug, running my hand through the sand.

"I honestly don't remember. Two weeks ago, maybe? Week before that?"

Shock widens her eyes, and her mouth drops open slightly.

"Are you serious? Why in the world are you not surfing every day? You live literally right there."

I smile and shrug again. "I guess whenever I have a moment where I could, I usually end up talking myself out of it. My to-do list is typically pretty long." She shakes her head slowly, fixing her gaze back out at the ocean.

"That's a true shame," she says quietly, like what I said makes her truly sad.

"What about you?" I ask, trying to prolong our time together now that we're done surfing.

"I surfed for a while the day after I got back from my trip, but I haven't since. Got busy with wedding stuff." She straightens her legs out, pressing her hands into the sand behind her, tilting her face toward the sun.

"Spain, right? That's where you were?"

"Yup." Her eyes light up when she brings them back to me. "It was amazing. Have you ever been?"

The laugh that comes out of me is louder than I mean for it to be as I scratch just above my eyebrow.

"Why is that funny?" Playfulness shines behind her eyes as she gently pushes my bicep. A small shiver runs through me from her touch, and I know that, without a doubt, I'm enjoying the contact more than I should.

"I've actually never been out of the Hawaiian islands," I tell her honestly.

"Stop." Her eyes widen again.

"It's true," I chuckle.

"No way." Her gaze stays locked on me.

"I'm serious." My smile grows wider as I watch her eyes glaze over in disbelief, a flash of pity becoming apparent.

"That's literally a life that I can't imagine," she muses. "How come?"

"Well, when I was growing up, we had every intention to go somewhere as a family. It was just a matter of saving up for a trip." I clear my throat. "My mom started a vacation fund in an old jar that she and my dad put cash in every time they brought a paycheck home. Her dream was to take us to Disney World. My dad wanted to go to Mexico. Anyway, when he left, my mom had no choice but to put that money toward bills. Then, I got a job. Then, a second job. Then, I started my own business, so I guess traveling just wasn't a priority anymore." I run my hands through my wet hair and glance at her.

"I'm sorry," she says sincerely, holding my stare for an extra beat. "Have you heard from your dad at all?"

"Nah. Not even once since he left. I don't expect him to reach out, though, so I don't get disappointed. It just is what it is."

"That's a really hard thing for a son to go through. Losing a dad." Her expression gets cloudy, and I wonder if she's thinking about me or herself and John.

"It was," I admit. "But honestly, it made me the man I am today. And showed me the perfect example of the man I never want to be. Plus, if he hadn't left, I would have never gone over to your house the next day to take my mind off everything. I was hoping that hanging with John would help my mood, but really it was your dance performance that you forced us to watch that really cheered me up," I laugh, remembering the pink fuzzy crown on her head and the ridiculously short ballerina skirt she had on over her pants.

"Really?" Her face lights up with excitement, and she lets

out a laugh before turning serious. "I did that for you, you know. The performance."

"What do you mean?" I stretch all the way out onto my side, leaning up on my forearm, resting my head on my shoulder to look up at her.

"You and John were too serious. I didn't know at that point what had happened, but I immediately thought it was my duty to make you guys laugh. Man, I was ridiculous sometimes." She huffs a small laugh.

"No, that's really cute. And it worked—for a while, at least. Anyway," I say with a shake of my head, "it's all good. I don't need to travel. I'm content where I am."

She gives me the softest of smiles, with a knowing hint in her eyes—a look that I haven't seen before from her. One that says she can see through me. That she just might be seeing parts of me that everyone else looks past. It makes my heart beat just a touch faster. After a minute, she clears her throat.

"You know what I think?" she asks.

"What's that?" I raise my eyebrows at her as she wipes some sand off the top of her right knee.

"I think that maybe you don't do enough for yourself," she says quietly and cautiously.

"And why's that?" My eyes find and trail a catamaran off in the distance, not at all offended by her statement.

"I mean, I'm probably totally overstepping here…but for as long as I've known you, you've been the go-to guy that everyone can count on. The reliable one, right? Like checking on John's house when he's out of town. Or taking Matt and Elliot snorkeling at the drop of a hat. I know you've helped Matt at the bar with the renovations. You're always doing stuff for other people. All that, plus your business. Your family. It's a lot."

"You sound like my ex," I chuckle, but not with much power behind it, because I know she's right.

"Hey, I didn't say it was a bad thing." She dips her head a little to force eye contact. "Honestly. I've always thought it was sweet how you show up and take care of your people. It says a lot about your character." The corner of her mouth twists up in a gentle smile.

"You just gotta make sure you're taking care of yourself, too," she says quietly. "You're allowed to say no every once in a while, you know. To be more selfish."

I huff a laugh because she has no idea how hard it actually is for me to say no. Just the thought of turning someone down goes against every fiber in my body.

"I could definitely be better at saying no," I admit. She gives me a gentle, knowing smile.

"Anyway," she says in a more chipper voice, "I'm done rambling. Just want to make sure you're good."

"So, was this what you had in mind today?" I gesture at the ocean, effectively changing the subject. "We didn't really explore, but was this enough adventure for you?"

Her grin takes up her whole face as she takes a deep breath, staring off at the ocean with an expression that shows that whatever she's thinking about gives her peace.

"This was perfect." She nods. "Except, I think I'm ready for round two." She stands, dusts the sand off the backs of her legs, and reaches for her board.

"You up for it?" she yells back at me, already knee-deep in the water.

I shake my head and smile as I stand, knowing there's nothing else I'd rather be doing.

9

QUINN

"Okay, so definitely check out Poor Knights Island for some amazing scuba diving, and then if you're an adrenaline junkie like me, you absolutely must go jet boating in Taupō," I say to the group of tourists as I set the fourth mai tai next to the napkin where I had written my New Zealand travel recommendations. "It's unreal. They take you right to the base of Huka Falls, this absolutely stunning waterfall, and do three-sixties in this jet boat. Crazy fun."

"That sounds terrifying." The woman with the blonde fishtail braid laughs. "But thank you for the tips! Can't wait to start planning our next trip. I love that we ran into somebody who's actually been there."

"How about we focus on our current vacation? The one that we're on?" The man to her right laughs, rubbing his hand affectionately across her upper back.

"You're right." She smiles back at him. "Oahu is amazing.

And I'm having the best time with all of you. I just can't help it, though. Each trip just makes me more excited to plan the next one."

"You're a woman after my own heart," I laugh, clutching my chest. "I'm happy to help. Oh, I wrote down some of my favorite restaurants, too," I say, pointing to the napkin.

"Perfect, thank you."

"Absolutely. Anyway, enjoy your mai tais. I'll be back to check on you in a few minutes."

I grab a few empty glasses and a crumb-laden appetizer plate at a nearby high-top as I weave my way through tables on my way to the bar. Matt's behind the counter, shaking a martini, slightly shaking his head at me in amusement.

"Making new friends again?" he asks with a knowing smirk.

"Of course," I say as I set the empty glasses on the counter.

"Thought so," he says matter-of-factly.

"Isn't that the best way to go through life, though?" I ask, reveling in the rush I get from connecting with other people. "Finding common ground and similar interests with people you meet? Sharing life tidbits and tips you've picked up along the way, in the off chance that it'll be useful to them somehow on their own journey?" I stop myself, realizing that I'm rambling.

"Well, I wasn't trying to get that philosophical," he laughs, pouring the martini into a martini glass, "but I guess you're right. That's what makes you a great waitress, you know." He sets two cocktails on a tray and slides it toward me.

"Thanks," I say smugly, grabbing the tray and heading through the front doors out onto the outdoor patio that's currently under construction. I sidestep the main sign that says *Matt's Beach Bar* and another one that says *Excuse our mess—remodel in progress*.

This place used to be Marty's Beach Bar until Marty retired and sold it to Matt recently. He's been doing a lot of updating and remodeling, including this spacious patio that's almost finished except for one corner that still needs a few boards and a coat of sealant.

I veer toward the side that's finished and approach one of the tables that are settled under the canopy where a young couple is seated at an angle with a perfect view of the ocean.

"One martini and one spicy margarita." I place the drinks on the table in front of them. "Anything else I can get you two?"

"Should we do an appetizer, honey?" the woman asks, leaning closer to the man, sliding her hand across his thigh. He smiles intently back at her, looking adorably in love, making me wonder if they're on their honeymoon and where they might be from. I wonder what their story is, how and when they met, and what their family members are like.

"Sure, how about some chicken nachos?" he asks, still staring deep into her eyes.

"You got it," I say when the woman agrees. I make my way in through the doors, the empty tray hanging by my side. Admittedly, serving at a bar isn't necessarily my idea of a dream job, but I have to say, I don't hate it for the time being. I don't mind getting to meet and chat with so many people throughout the course of a shift. In fact, I absolutely love that part. Discovering where people are from, what they're here for, and where they're heading next. It fuels my soul when I'm not actually traveling myself.

"Can you ring up an order for chicken nachos, please?" I ask Matt as I lean against the counter.

"Sure thing," he says, keying some numbers into the touch screen on the monitor to his right. He just upgraded and installed the bar's point-of-sale system last week, which included these new monitors. John and I used to come here as kids when it was Marty's. It was the best place to get a virgin-blended strawberry daiquiri after playing on the beach for hours. This place holds some fond childhood memories for me, but it's been especially fun now watching Matt turn it into the bar of his dreams.

When he finishes keying in the order, he checks his watch. "Hey, why don't you take your break? You're about due. I'll run the nachos out when they're ready."

"Sure, that would be great. Thanks. Be back in twenty." I head down the hall, past the bathrooms and the construction buckets filled with gear, and take a right into the small break room at the end of the hallway. The chair swivels slightly as I sit and reach under the desk where I shoved my white sling bag. I grab my phone and a peanut-butter protein bar, zipper the bag shut and lean back into the chair. When I turn my phone upright, I notice that I have two unread text messages.

Brian: Wanted you to know that my buddy Eric asked me to come help him work on the old Jeep he's fixing up, and I said I couldn't—even though I absolutely could.

Brian: Thought you'd be proud.

A grin stretches across my face as I take a bite of my bar and slowly push my foot against the floor to turn the chair back and forth, ignoring the warmth in my chest that just appeared.

Quinn: *Gasp* I'm SO proud! How does it feel to say no for once?

Brian: Terrible. I feel guilty. He's working on it all by himself.

Quinn: Don't feel guilty! I'm sure he can manage just fine without you this one time. What are you gonna do with your newfound 'me time'?

Brian: Probably go check on my mom's house. To keep my mind off the guilt.

Quinn: Brian Sanderson. You will not.

Brian: Kidding.

I huff a small laugh to myself. Who knew I would get such enjoyment from talking to Brian? Or hanging out with him, for that matter. Surfing with him earlier today was exactly what I needed to get me out of my dream slump. The heaviness had melted away relatively quickly. And it wasn't just from the surfing, either. It was also from talking with him on the beach. Just being there, sitting next to him in the sand. It was the perfect distraction, and one I wholeheartedly needed.

Quinn: Thanks again for keeping me company earlier. I appreciate it.

Brian: No prob. It was nice—you're fun to be around.

The protein bar pauses in the air midway to my mouth. *You're fun to be around.* What does he mean by that? And why do I like it so much? My heart starts beating just a touch faster, and I chide myself for being one of those girls. The girls who fall head over heels for a good-looking guy the second he smiles in her direction. The ones who are practically planning out their entire future before dinner gets cold on their first date. No, I refuse to let that happen. That's just not me.

I really like Brian, and honestly, I have always thought he was attractive. I mean, look at the guy—a surfer bum with a deep tan, strong physique and tattoos, who's also the biggest sweetheart I've ever known. What's not to like? But I don't do long-term relationships. Period. Never have. So, there's no point in even entertaining the brother's-best-friend boundary line that I probably shouldn't even be crossing anyway.

It wouldn't be worth it to potentially risk making John mad

or messing up the friendship Brian and I have if I already know it won't be going anywhere. I blow out a sigh and slide my phone back into my bag, leaving our conversation at that. I pop the last bite of the bar into my mouth and head out of the break room, doing my best to shift my focus away from thoughts of Brian.

"There she is!" a loud, booming voice calls out when I round the corner. I look up and break out into a grin when I see two of my favorite locals sitting on the other side of the bar.

"Frank. Carlos," I say in greeting, walking along the inside of the bar until I'm standing in front of the two elderly friends. "You two are here early today."

"Yeah, the wives had their first joint tennis lesson this afternoon, so we snuck out of the neighborhood early," Frank says, his skin wrinkling as he smiles, a dead giveaway of both his age and the lifetime he's had in the Hawaiian sun. "Although, nosy Nancy was outside gardening when we met in front of Carlos' house, so she probably ratted us out already."

"Well, you better enjoy those beers while you can, then." I wink.

"That's the spirit," Carlos agrees, clanking his frosted mug with Frank's.

"You've got a new table in your section," Matt says quietly, coming behind me to grab a seltzer out of the mini fridge on my right.

"Sounds good," I reply, then turn to the men. "Enjoy, gentlemen. Don't get into any trouble over here, alright?"

"You know we can't make any promises like that, sweetheart," Frank says as I break out into a grin and start walking to the other side of the bar. I grab a small stack of cocktail napkins and my ordering pad and head onto the floor to finish out the rest of my afternoon shift.

10

QUINN

"Coming!" I shout at my door when I hear a knock for the second time. Shuffling my feet down the hallway, I pass the kitchen and living room, going as fast as I can while pulling my hair back in a ponytail. When I swing the door open, my mouth drops partially open in surprise. Brian's standing with his hands in the pockets of his black basketball shorts, rocking slightly forward on the balls of his feet.

"Brian. Hey," I mumble, momentarily distracted by his dark eyes that are piercing directly into mine.

"Hey," he says, pushing one side of his mouth up into a smirk, deepening that darn dimple again. "You busy? My morning charter canceled last minute…and I want to take you somewhere."

"You want to take me somewhere?" I repeat slowly, thoroughly confused by what's happening. Brian has never once, in all the years I've known him, shown up at my apartment by himself, without John. But I guess the same could be said for me showing up at his house the other day when we surfed.

"Yeah." He nods, looking at me expectantly. "I want to show you something."

A rush of excitement runs up my spine, and without permission, butterflies start to flutter in my stomach.

"Okay…right now?" I ask.

"Yes. If you're not busy, of course. And if you want to come?" He suddenly looks unsure.

"Sure, I'll come." I smile, feeling my pulse quicken at the mere thought of this unknown adventure. "Let me grab my purse."

"Bring your camera, too," he calls after me, staying firmly planted in my doorway.

"Ooh, my camera? Please tell me you're going to pose for me somewhere. You'd seriously be the perfect model."

He chuckles, running his hand through his thick wavy hair, a chunk falling across his forehead, which only further confirms my statement.

"I'm gonna brush over the fact that you called me a model for now, but I'll remember that one later," he says with a twinkle in his eye. "And no, I will not be posing for you."

"Darn." I move past him, camera bag in hand, pulling the door shut behind me.

"So, where are you taking me, then?" I ask as we head down the stairs toward the front door of the apartment building.

"Well, I'm sure you've already been there many times, but I want to take you to the Halona Blowhole. The daily reports say the tide should be extra high this morning, so I figured the blowhole would be something cool to photograph. Get some practice anyway?"

I gasp a breath, a warmth spreading in my chest at his thoughtfulness. "Oh! That's a great idea, Brian!"

I spot his white truck in the first row of parking spaces in the lot. He walks half a step ahead of me to reach for the passenger-side door before I do. I give him a smile as he holds the door open for me to climb in, then shuts it gently behind me. I can't seem to wipe the smile from my face as he jogs around the back of the truck to the driver's side.

"Alright. Let's go," his husky voice vibrates close to my ear as he places a hand on the back of my seat, twisting to look behind him as he reverses. I put my feet up on the dash and roll down the window, settling in for the drive.

"So, let me get this straight." I peer over at him. "You were just looking through the daily tide chart and thought, *Hey, that reminds me of Quinn?*"

"Pretty much," he laughs. "After my charter canceled, I was trying to plan out my day. I took your advice and was trying to come up with something I could do that was 'selfish,' as you say. That thought process reminded me of you. Then, I saw the tide chart, and the rest is history."

"As much as I totally appreciate what you're doing, you know this doesn't count, right? This isn't selfish at all. You're doing this for me," I say pointedly.

"Not necessarily. It's partially selfish on my part." The confidence in his voice does something to my stomach. "I wanted to do this."

I bite my lip to stop the rogue smile that's threatening to spread too big.

"Still doesn't count." My voice comes out just above a whisper.

As we drive along the scenic Kalaniana'ole Highway, I take my camera out of the case and capture a few shots of the coastline as we pass by. One image of a passing cluster of palm trees. Another of some boulders that line a cliff that juts out into the ocean in the distance. I shift in my seat to focus my camera on Brian, the row of rocks that the road runs alongside whizzing past in the backdrop. His left arm is bent, resting outside the open window, holding his head up. The wind ruffles the edges of his already-tousled dark hair. His right arm is straight, hand clutching the top of the steering wheel. I take a couple shots of his profile, the tattoos that cascade down his arm on full display.

"I thought I said I wasn't gonna be your model?" He smiles as he peers over at me.

"Joke's on you, I guess," I murmur, adjusting the exposure before bringing the camera back up to my face. I focus in on the skull that's barely emerging from under his T-shirt sleeve. An intricate mix of waves, circular patterns, and flower petals wrap around the skull and run all the way down to his wrist. I study each one, wondering if there's any particular meaning behind any of them.

"Are you done?" he laughs, switching hands on the wheel so the one closest to me can reach across to block the camera.

"Ugh, fine," I sigh and straighten myself out on the seat. "You know, if this whole fishing business doesn't pan out, you really could totally make it in the modeling industry. You have excellent bone structure."

He snorts while turning on his turn signal. "Not a chance."

"I'm just saying," I say with a shrug, noticing that we're finally pulling into the parking area.

We both hop out and walk side by side toward the overlook platform. The blowhole is visible instantly, and even though I have seen it many times before, a thrill runs through me when water sprays up from the hole. The structure is formed by lava tubes made from volcanic eruptions thousands of years ago. When the tide and the wind are just right, it can shoot water up to thirty feet in the air.

I lift my camera and capture the impressive spray of water, moving to change the angle so that the ocean is the backdrop. When it settles back down, I take a few of just the blowhole itself, wind ripping through my hair at the same time. When the next shot of water sprays up, I capture an image with a massive wave crashing up onto the rocky ledge behind it, two different swells rocketing up high. I look at the image on the display screen, and a rush of gratification runs through me. I love the feeling I get when I capture the image just right. When it turns out exactly the way I see it in my mind.

I lower the camera and can see Brian in my peripheral vision, standing behind my shoulder, patiently waiting and watching me. His presence is a strong, steady one that's almost palpable. He's not rushing me at all, just watching, completely content to wait however long he needs to until I'm satisfied. I smile to myself, fully acknowledging his support and feeling special that his attention is solely focused on me.

"Wanna go down to the cove?" I turn to ask him, hoping he'll want to hike down the trail on the other side of the parking lot to get to Halona Beach Cove. Once again, I'm taken aback by the intensity of his warm eyes as they meet mine, his expression unreadable.

"Let's do it," he says quietly with a nod, his stare holding mine for an extra beat. He backs up slowly, then turns the opposite direction.

We cross the mostly empty parking lot and find the unmarked path that will take us down into the cove. The path is rough—mostly jagged lava rock that we'll need to hike down. Brian goes in front of me and turns back to offer his hand. When I slip my hand in his, he immediately clasps his hand firmly around mine. I mentally roll my eyes at myself and the shiver that involuntarily runs down my spine. I wonder why I've never noticed the chemistry that's been sparking between us, because it seems so obvious now. So intense.

I don't feel the need to tell him that I once spent the entire week of my spring break in college rock climbing in Boulder, Colorado. I can easily handle this on my own. But I guess maybe I don't want to. Maybe I like the feel of my hand in his. I like seeing this protective side of him that's directed at me.

When we reach the clearing of sand at the bottom, I pause next to him and take in the stunning view. The cove is one of Oahu's somewhat secluded beaches, surrounded by large cliffs of lava rock, barely visible from the road that runs right above. A narrow opening between two rock clusters is where the turquoise water of the ocean crashes onto shore. There's usually a scattering of tourists filling the cove, but I'm thankful that it's just us for now. Our own little slice of paradise.

Brian releases my hand suddenly, as if he just remembered that he was still holding it. He lifts his shirt above his head, exposing his muscular frame, leaving him in just his basketball shorts. I match the smile he flashes at me, walk ahead of him, and widen my arms at my side like I'm showcasing the whole cove.

"Let's go explore!"

11

BRIAN

John.
John.
John.

The reminder to myself that Quinn is my best friend's little sister does very little to quell my wandering, borderline inappropriate thoughts. There's no question that I should definitely not be wondering how soft her lips are or what it would feel to slide my fingers through her hair as I push her up against one of these rocks. Or down onto the sand.

Thoughts like these have been lingering with me all day, despite my best effort to make them disappear. I dip my head, smile, and follow Quinn as she frolics along the water's edge, her feet splashing with each step. The waves rush over our feet, surging across the sand, and dissipating into a white-ish foam before retreating back toward the ocean. With the wind being considerably weaker down here, the heat from the sun warms the left side of my face as I follow her.

"Feel like climbing that cliff over there?" she challenges me with a daredevil look in her eyes, continuing her way to the far edge of the cove. I try hard to dial down the protective urge that suddenly hits me. I don't want to be a drag, but I definitely don't like the idea of her climbing that sharp-edged cliff.

"You don't have the right shoes." I point to her flip-flops, attempting to talk her out of it.

"So?" Her grin only grows wider, a challenge burning in her eyes.

"That rock could be slippery." My feeble comeback only makes the resolve stronger on her face.

"Only one way to find out." She wiggles her eyebrows. "Besides, you'll catch me if I fall, right?" She reaches the rock wall and pauses, looking up at every pointed edge to determine the best course.

"Well, yeah, obviously." I sigh, resigning to the fact that she's not really listening to what I'm saying.

"You don't have to come if you're scared," she teases, throwing a look my way behind her shoulder. Only she can tease me, be completely intent on pushing me out of my safety zone, and still be so damn endearing somehow.

"I can't spot you if I'm climbing," I point out, sliding my hands into my pockets again.

"Good call. I'll go first, and then I can spot you."

"Sure. Just be careful, okay?"

"Yes, sir," she says, already two steps up. The rock has a gradual incline to it, and she makes her way slowly up, taking her time to feel for a sturdy spot to put her foot next. To my relief, she seems to be cautious, carefully deciding each step. I take the opportunity to watch her unabashedly, my eyes roaming over every inch of her.

Her hair is pulled back into a low, twisted bun, and her

maroon swimsuit is visible from the side of her loose, gray tank top. She's wearing black athletic shorts that slide up her thigh a little higher every time she hoists her toned legs up to the next rock. I can see from this angle that she's biting her lip in concentration, and I force myself to look away because that most definitely is not helping to quell my thoughts.

Eventually, she makes it to a flatter stretch of rock and stands, turning around toward the ocean, steadying herself with a hand on the rock wall behind her.

"Ah, it's so beautiful!" she calls down to me, shielding the sun with her hand. I have no desire to follow her gaze out toward the water, so instead, I keep my gaze on her, wholeheartedly convinced that my view is better.

"Are you done now?" I shout to be heard over the loud waves crashing on my left.

She giggles with a slight shake of her head, but she turns around and starts her descent down while I anxiously watch every step. When she gets closer to the bottom, she loses her footing and lets out a yelp. I let out a gasp as I move closer, bracing myself to catch her if she falls. The laugh that comes out of her is not what I expect to hear next.

"I'm okay. I'm just kidding!" she says guiltily and makes eye contact while I sigh and put my hands on my hips. "You're kind of adorable when you're mad, do you know that?"

My mouth lifts up into a smirk, and I shake my head from side to side. I refuse to move back to give her space until I know she's on stable ground. It's only when she steps onto the sand and turns around that I register how close to me she is. She pauses, as if frozen, her face directly in line with my chest, her own chest rising and falling with her breath. I watch as her eyes slowly rise up until they meet mine, any trace of playfulness gone. The air sparks between us, and I can't bring myself to look away.

"You want to climb?" she asks with a slightly shaky voice. I can only give a slight shake of my head, not able to form words. The close proximity to her body has rendered my brain completely useless.

"Brian," she mutters my name, half a question, half a statement.

"Hmm," I hum in response, my head involuntarily dipping slightly lower. She takes a small step closer to me, and I can feel my heart pounding, goosebumps running across the top of my skin. Her eyes remain glued to mine, shifting back and forth slowly as if she's searching for something.

"Has anyone ever told you that you have really intense eyes?" she breathes, lifting her chin, her voice just above a whisper.

"No." I shake my head slightly, my gaze flicking to her lips, which she just bit the corner of.

John.
John.
John.

His name makes me momentarily pause, but it's forgotten without a trace the second she leans up on the tips of her toes to press her lips to mine. My stomach lurches, and I immediately bring both of my hands gently to her neck, my thumbs resting softly on each side of her jaw, the tips of my fingers curling around the back of her neck. She places her hands on the sides of my torso just above my waist, digging her fingers into my skin. She tilts her head to deepen the kiss and slides her hands around and up my back, pressing them flat against me. I move closer until my stomach is pressed to hers. A shiver runs down my spine at the touch, and I relish in the high of kissing her.

John.
John.

John.

This time, his name jolts me back to reality, and I pull my mouth from hers, but still, my body refuses to let go of the rest of her. I keep my hands around her face and bring my forehead to rest on hers.

"Quinn…what are we doing?" I say breathlessly, guilt creeping all the way in.

"Kissing," she says matter-of-factly and smiles, to which I burst out a laugh.

"I'm aware of that," I say through a chuckle. I reluctantly take a step back, dropping my hands to my sides.

"What are we doing?" I repeat softly.

She takes a deep breath in and releases it slowly.

"I don't know." She lifts her shoulders up in a shrug, and the playfulness from earlier returns when she smiles. "Having fun?"

I scratch at the back of my neck and stare down at the sand, weighing the consequences of our actions. What will John think? This is Quinn. I've known her almost my entire life. Did I just ruin our friendship and my friendship with John, messing everything up for our whole friend group?

"Hey," she says softly, stepping closer to me. "Don't overthink it, okay? It's all good, Brian, I promise." I look up to find her focusing on me.

"Listen…I've learned along the way that it's better to go through life without a ton of expectations. To not overanalyze— just do. Fly by the seat of your pants and all that. Go with what feels right in the moment. It's easier that way. Less pressure." She closes the gap between us and then grabs my hand, entwining her fingers with mine.

"And what about your brother?" I ask, pointing out the very obvious elephant in the cove.

She cringes and then shrugs. "It's not that I don't care what he thinks, because I do. I just don't live my life for anyone else,

Brian, including him. Besides, it was just a kiss, right? This doesn't have to ruin any of our relationships. Let's just have fun," she suggests. "Keep it light."

I bite the inside of my cheek and mull over her words very carefully until eventually, I squeeze her hand and shoot her a smile.

"I like the sound of that," I agree. I untangle our hands, bringing my arm around her shoulder to turn us around. I squeeze gently and kiss the side of her head as we start walking toward the other side of the cove. I'm still not completely convinced that I shouldn't regret that kiss, but for now, I'm choosing to focus on how amazing it was.

"Come on, let's head back."

12

QUINN

"Here's the fruit bowl." I place my contribution in the middle of the low-sitting boho picnic table that's set up on top of a large blanket on the beach. There are seven light-blue and white place settings surrounding the perimeter of the table, with various other coastal-hued utensils and serving bowls laid out in the center.

"Perfect!" says Mia, bending over to move the bowl of pasta salad over slightly to make more room for my fruit bowl.

"I'm so happy you're back. I missed you guys," I tell her, straightening to stand, smoothing my hands down the front of my jean shorts, then checking to make sure my loose white tank top is still tucked in the front of it.

"Me too! Our honeymoon was amazing, of course, but I gotta say, it's nice to be back. Did we miss anything while we were gone?"

"Nope. Same old," I tell her, sneaking a glance over at Brian, who's throwing the football with John and Matt.

I decided against telling her about kissing him two days ago. Not yet, anyway. I need to figure out if that was a one-time-only thing or if it's going to happen again. I have to admit, I'm hoping there'll be a repeat occurrence. I still get a rush of butterflies when I think about kissing him. The way his hands gently cradled my face, like I was the most precious thing he's ever held. The way his stomach was pressed to mine, his tall, muscular frame completely overshadowing mine.

Yup, that was a top-tier kiss, that's for sure. The anticipation of another one is absolutely killing me. But our interactions since then have been minimal. When he dropped me off at my apartment that day, I planted a quick kiss on his cheek before hopping out of his truck. Then, he sent me a picture while I was working at the coffee shop yesterday of the massive amberjack that one of his charter guests caught. Brief text exchanges here and there are the only contact we've had until today. When Mia sent out the details for this post-honeymoon beach picnic in a group text, I was excited when Brian said he would be here. I've been looking forward to seeing him. I just didn't anticipate how distracting he'd be without a shirt on.

"It's annoying, isn't it?" Paige comes up next to me, Noelle on her hip, catching me looking at the guys. "How much muscle is in that group over there? I swear, surfing has got to be the best workout."

"Of course, it is—look at Quinn!" Mia pipes in, stuffing a chip in her mouth. "She has a bangin' body."

"Who has a bangin' body?" Matt asks, sneaking up on us with John and Brian close behind.

"Quinn does," Paige says nonchalantly. "We think it's the surfing." I catch Brian's eyes darting to mine, once again oozing with intensity, which makes my heart skip a beat.

"Okay, stop," I laugh it off, waving my hand in Paige's general direction, feeling my cheeks start to flush.

"It's true." She shrugs.

If this exact conversation would have taken place a month ago, it wouldn't have affected me one bit. But now, I can't help but be hyper-aware of Brian's presence and get flustered at the thought that he might notice me like that.

"Alright, let's eat!" Mia says, gesturing to the table. I walk over and drop down on one of the flat tan pillows that Mia laid out around the perimeter of the table. Paige and Mia sit down on either side of me, and their husbands crouch next to them. Brian finds the spot directly across from me, and we share a quick smile when our eyes meet. Once again, the intensity of his dark eyes is distracting until Elliot bumps into him, forcing him to look away. Elliot places a hand on Brian's shoulder to steady himself and drops to the pillow next to Brian, across from Paige and Matt. When he's settled, he gestures for Matt to pass him his little sister. He perches Noelle on his lap and hands her a soft book to play with.

"So, Brian, tell me about the tournament again," John says, sliding the serving spoon back into the fruit bowl and passing it to him.

I watch as Brian uses the back of his hand to wipe at a chip crumb at the corner of his mouth before turning to John. "The Annual Blue Marlin Tournament details were posted yesterday. It's in four weeks. Cash prize of up to $100,000, depending on the size of the marlin we catch. It's a full-day commitment. I need three guys on my team. You in?"

"Hell yeah," John replies. "I missed out last year. Why didn't I do it again?"

"You were too busy being preoccupied with your new fiancée. No offense," Brian says, smiling at Mia, who shrugs her shoulders, unaffected.

"Matt, what about you? You in?" He turns to Matt.

"Paige? Am I in?" Matt throws his arm around her shoulders.

I snort a laugh, knowing full well that he doesn't need Paige's approval. He just wants it.

"Go ahead! Sounds fun," she replies, to which he answers with a kiss on her temple.

"You need three guys, right?" Elliot asks excitedly. "Can I be the third?"

Brian turns to ruffle his hair. "Sorry, big guy. You are my best fishing buddy, but the tournament rules say eighteen plus. I'll have to see if my friend, Eric, is interested."

The guys nod their heads in a silent agreement.

"Quinn, when's your next trip?" Mia turns her attention to me. "Where's the wind blowing you this time?"

"I don't have anything booked yet, unfortunately. I'll probably plan to go somewhere in a couple weeks. I'm dying to book something, but I haven't narrowed it down yet. Maybe Croatia or the Maldives." The familiar fire in my belly to get on a plane and fly somewhere—anywhere—started amping up the last few days. I feel antsy like this pretty frequently, always ready for another adventure. It really doesn't matter where I go, as long as it's a new place to explore.

"I can't believe you don't book farther in advance," Mia replies. "I would need so much time to plan everything out."

"I don't need to plan a whole lot when I travel," I say with a shrug, "It's just me, so I usually just go with the flow once I'm there. Plus, I can find some really amazing deals on airfare and lodging if I wait until last minute."

"That's smart," she says cheerfully. "You'll have to teach me your ways sometime."

The conversation shifts, and we continue with small talk as we finish eating.

"Alright, who's up for a game of flag football?" Matt asks as he gets up and starts throwing the dirty plates and utensils into a garbage bag.

"Me!" Elliot shouts, the rest of us chiming in as well. Mia offers to stay on the sidelines on a beach towel with Noelle, and the rest of us split onto the sand into teams.

"Go long!" John calls to me and throws a spiral down the beach, which I automatically sprint for but narrowly miss. I grab the football and jog back to the group.

"My bad," John apologizes with a grin. "Bad throw."

"What was that? Even I can throw better than that." I laugh as I line up next to Matt and Paige. Elliot, John, and Brian are on the opposing team and create a line across from us, the ocean to our right.

"Hut," Matt calls out, and Paige and I scatter, attempting to dodge the other team. Elliot tries to block me, but I manage to go wide and avoid his attempted tackle. Matt passes to Paige, but John intercepts, catching the ball and then charging past Matt and the imaginary end zone, throwing the ball into the sand in victory.

"Aw, it's alright," Matt consoles Paige, bringing her in for a hug, "I wanted you on my team for your looks, not your talent."

I laugh when Paige slaps him on the chest, pushing him away from her playfully.

"Alright, let's try this again," Matt says.

This time, when we break, I run through the center, glancing back just in time to see Matt throw the ball straight for me. I catch it firmly with a thud, bringing it close to my side until I feel two strong, visibly inked arms grab me from behind, just above my waist.

I let out a squeal as Brian lifts my feet up in the air, my weight falling back on his chest, and he spins me around in a circle. When he brings me forward and sets me gently onto the sand, I mentally shake off the growing butterflies and snatch the ball from his grasp.

"Oh, it's on. Watch your back, old man," I tease, walking backward toward my team, getting momentarily sucked into his stare, which is only slightly overshadowed by the distracting grin on his face.

"I'd like to see you try," he says slyly in a challenge.

John throws a spiral to Brian, who runs wide. Despite my best effort to stop him, he sideswipes me at the last second but not before I jump on his back, wrapping my arms around the top of his shoulder and my legs around his waist. I use all my weight to try and get him to buckle, but he just effortlessly runs across the end zone with me glued to his back as if I didn't hinder him in the slightest.

He drops the ball and brings both hands up to grip my thighs. I yelp as he tightens his grip and starts tickling. I free myself and jump down off of him, a rush of adrenaline running through me from the contact. I shake my head with a smile, attempting to shake off the buzz. We keep playing for the next half hour or so until Noelle starts fussing and the rest of us are all officially out of breath.

"Alright, we gotta head home. Time for her nap," Matt says, shaking hands with both the guys.

"See ya," I tell Paige, giving her a hug. "Hey, let me know next time you and Mia go hiking. I'd love to tag along."

"Will do. We were talking about going this weekend," she says, joining Matt, Elliot, and Noelle to gather their things. With a final wave, they start walking off the beach as I turn to help finish picking up.

"Oh, don't worry about it, Quinn," Mia says. "John and I are going to stay for a little while, so we'll get the rest of this. You go ahead."

"Okay, sounds good," I say, giving both Mia and John a hug goodbye.

"I'm leaving, too. I'll walk with you," Brian says casually, shaking John's hand before joining me as we venture toward the parking lot. I look down at the sand that's seeping farther between my toes with each step, my sandals hanging from my hand at my side.

"So, what do you have going on the next couple days?" he asks me as we walk widely around a cluster of lounge chairs.

"Not much. I'll probably hang out with Tori tomorrow. She has the day off, so we might meet up. What about you?"

"I'll drop by my mom's on my way home from here to check in. Paperwork stuff for the boat tonight, then I have a full-day charter booked for tomorrow," he says as we reach my car. He pulls the door open for me, then pauses while he rolls his lips.

"See you soon?" he says thickly. It comes out as a mix of a question and a plea. I bite at the corner of my lip and smile, butterflies coming alive in my stomach.

"Sure."

13

BRIAN

"Come on, Ethan, let's go," I say for the third time as Ethan finally comes out of the bathroom and moseys down the hallway toward where I'm not so patiently waiting by my front door.

"I'm coming, man," he mutters under his breath while rubbing at his eyes. "Sleeping is a basic human right, you know. Waking up this early is just cruel."

"Not if you want a job on my boat. I can't help that the fish bite the best in the morning. Besides, it's 5:30, not the middle of the night. Plenty of people wake up this early." I wait for him to pass, then close the door behind me and follow him down the path around the side of my house.

"What time did you get in last night, anyway?" I ask, lifting a stray palm tree branch out of the way.

I can see the back of his shoulders lift up in a shrug. "I dunno. Sometime around midnight, I think."

Once we're settled inside my truck, I start heading down my

short driveway.

"Does Mom know you slept at my place?"

"She probably figured it out. Not that she'd care either way," he says in a low mumble.

"Hey, that's not fair." I shoot him a sideways glance.

"Well, it's the truth."

A knot starts to form in my stomach. I hate that their relationship is strained, and I wish there was more I could do to make it better. She's at a loss for how to connect with him, and he's too stubborn to make an effort. I'm just stuck in the middle, trying my best to help them get along.

"You know, it wouldn't hurt for you to be a little nicer to her. I know she wasn't around a lot when you were growing up, but she got dealt a shitty hand. She did the best she could." I come to a stop sign, flip my turn signal on, and turn right, taking us on the same route to the marina that I take every single day and could probably drive with my eyes closed by now. "That's not saying I don't think you were dealt a shitty hand, too. You definitely deserved better. But you only get one mom in life, Ethan. And you know what? She's here. She's trying. That's more than we can say about Dad."

A huff is all I get in return as he crosses his arms and stares out the window, burrowing his head farther inside the hood of his sweatshirt. When his phone dings in his pocket, he pulls it out and starts typing.

"Who the hell's texting you this early?" I ask.

"Scotty," he mumbles. We drive the rest of the way to the marina in silence. When we arrive, he helps me haul some gear and a case of water down the stairs and onto the dock. At the boat, we get started on prepping it for the charter. Ethan sorts through and checks the rods, reels, and artificial bait that we'll use in addition to the shrimp we'll catch for bait on our way out. I'm flipping through the contract and fishing licenses when I hear footsteps on the dock.

"Hey." John waves as he strolls down the dock slip toward us, looking like he just walked straight out of the ocean in his swim trunks and barely dry skin.

"What's goin' on, man?" I ask, feeling a small flutter of nerves rise up. Seeing him brings up mixed feelings. He's one of the people I'm the closest to in my life, and it's always good to see him, but I've been meaning to have a conversation with him, and I'm not confident about how it will go, which is making me a little uneasy.

"I was up early teaching a sunrise surf lesson and didn't want to head back to the house just yet. Mia's still struggling with jet lag, and I don't want to wake her. Figured I'd drop by to see if you were around." He hops in the boat and takes a seat on the bench. "Looks like great weather today for fishing, huh?"

"Yeah, just getting prepped and ready for an eight-hour trip." I hesitate, then blow out a breath, figuring now is as good a time as any to rip off the Band-aid. "Listen, I was actually planning to call you after I finished today. I, uh…I want to talk to you about something."

He's quiet for a minute and somehow doesn't seem surprised as he stares at me, his eyes locked on mine. "Is this about Quinn?"

My stomach drops the same way it always did as a kid when you knew you were about to get grounded—or at least a stern lecturing. I can't help but brace myself for the possibility of getting chewed out. I clear my throat and yell to Ethan at the front of the boat.

"Hey, Ethan. Can you run back up to my truck and grab the extra phone charger?" He doesn't bother to give me a response, just silently does what I ask. When he's out of earshot, I move to sit next to John.

"So, I guess Mia was right," he starts before I have a chance. "She mentioned that she noticed there was some 'flirty vibes'—her words, not mine—between you two at the picnic and—"

"I kissed her," I blurt out, cutting him off, not able to hold it in any longer. Whichever way this is going to go, I figure he might as well know the whole truth. John winces and makes a face like he's thoroughly disgusted and nauseated at the same time. "Listen, I'm sorry, man. I didn't mean for it to happen. I was helping her with her photography stuff, and we started spending more time together while you were on your honeymoon. It just sort of happened…I totally understand if you want to punch me right now."

He runs his hand over his jaw, and dread runs through me as each second passes with us sitting in silence.

"Do you like her?" he finally asks quietly.

It surprises me how quickly the word yes sits at the tip of my tongue. I've tried to tone down or suppress any thoughts or feelings that creep up when I think about her because of what John might think, but when I do allow myself to really think about it—yes. I like her. I like her a lot.

"I do," I say guiltily with a cringe, and I watch as he blows out a low breath.

"My sister? Really?" He scratches vigorously at his jaw.

"But if it's crossing a line or is too weird for you in any way, then this is the end of it. I give you my word."

John shakes his head slightly. "Listen, man," he starts slowly, "I can't say it doesn't gross me out, and I definitely don't want to know details…but I know far too well that life is too short. You never know what's gonna happen tomorrow, so I'm all about doing what makes you happy. I can try and get used to it. I would never tell you or Quinn not to pursue something if that's what you both want to do."

Relief rushes through me, and I allow myself to feel a little bit of the excitement that's creeping up my spine.

"Thanks, man. I really appreciate that." I hold my hand out for John to shake, which he reciprocates with a firm grasp.

"But I gotta warn you," he says, "I don't really see where

this'll go. She doesn't do long-term relationships. Never has. I think the longest relationship was a month or two. She tends to eat guys up and spit them out," he laughs, peering at me, "so don't say I didn't warn you."

I chuckle, knowing full well what Quinn's opinion toward relationships is. The problem is, the feeling I get when I'm around her makes me not really care. I just want more of that feeling—even if it's only short-lived.

"I hear you," I smirk. "We'll see what happens, I guess. Thanks for being cool about this. I swear I wasn't trying to keep it from you."

"No worries," John says, standing when Ethan comes back in sight. "Just don't hurt her. I was her brother before I was your best friend. Remember that."

"I'm well aware. Last thing I want to do is piss you off," I laugh, venturing back to the stack of papers I was looking through. "What are you doing the rest of the day?" I ask, fully ready and grateful to change the subject and put this topic behind us.

"I've got a couple more surfing lessons to teach this afternoon. Mia's playing a lot of catch-up at work after being gone, so she'll be busy with that. Probably just taking it easy tonight." He shrugs. "Anyway, I'll let you get back to it. Have fun on your charter. See ya, Ethan." He throws a glance at Ethan before stepping over onto the dock. I give him a shrug when Ethan doesn't bother to turn around, instead throwing a casual peace sign up.

"See ya later, John," I call as he makes his way off the dock. I watch him go, relieved that that conversation is over with. I don't know what will happen, if anything, between me and Quinn, but a weight's been lifted now that I know that John's mostly okay with it. With a nod of my head, I go back to prepping the boat.

14

QUINN

"Here's your iced dirty chai latte." I smile at the woman as I hand her the coffee drink, then immediately mark the order as complete and jump into making the next drink order on the screen. I love the buzz of Julie's Coffee Shop and Juice Bar. The steady stream of people, the bustle of the employees behind the counter as we try and churn out the orders as fast as possible. Not to mention the aroma. Absolutely nothing beats the slightly nutty, yet perfectly sweet scent that hangs heavy in a coffee shop. It's a totally different vibe working here versus my shifts at Matt's bar, but I actually love the contrast between the two. Alternating between them keeps my life interesting.

"Thanks for helping this morning, Quinn," Julie says as she bags up a muffin next to me. "The customers always love when you're here."

"Oh, of course. Thanks for letting me pick up another shift this week. I'm glad you asked," I say, twisting to grab a straw and then placing the cup in a to-go carrier. I was only supposed to be on the schedule once this week, but Julie called late last night to see if I would be willing to fill in this morning for another employee who was sick.

"Hey, girl!" I smile at the familiar voice and turn to greet Tori, who's next in line. "Looking good in that apron."

"Thanks," I say in a chipper voice. "What can I get you?"

"I'll have a tall vanilla latte, please. And a report on when you're planning to see Brian next." She says the last part so fast that I do a double-take before sputtering out a laugh. I guess we're officially talking about this in public now. John sent me a text yesterday saying he knew about the kiss and that he was going to try his best to be cool with it. He also asked that I please not break Brian's heart.

Apparently, Mia noticed something between us at the picnic, which comes as absolutely no surprise. That girl's always trying to look for love connections and lives for a good love story. I was with Tori when John sent me the text, so I ended up spilling the beans to her as well. It's a little weird that everyone knows, especially since it's just a casual thing, but I guess now I don't have anything to feel guilty about. I'm excited to have some fun with him and see what happens.

"Easy, tiger. It's not a big deal," I say pointedly.

"Yeah, yeah, keeping it casual, that's what you said. I still can't believe you kissed Brian. I mean, it's Brian. He's friends with both of our brothers. We've literally known him forever." She lets out a deep sigh. "But at the same time, honestly, I don't blame you. Have you seen those tattoos? Girl, please." She fans herself like she's suddenly overheating. I roll my eyes and hand her the latte, my lips sealed.

"Alright, clearly, I'm not getting any more info here. Keep me updated!" She winks and smiles, sauntering back out the front door. I watch her as she leaves and take this moment of a lull between customers to text Brian.

Quinn: Hi! What are you up to today?

I could play hard to get and wait for him to reach out to me, but that's never really been my style. Where's the fun in that? I'm more of a take-the-bull-by-the-horns kind of girl.

Brian: Hey. I was just about to call you. I have a morning fishing charter, but it'll be done by noon. Want to hang this afternoon?

Quinn: Definitely. I can be at your place at one?

Brian: See ya then.

I slide my phone back into my apron with a smile on my face and turn to make myself a double espresso. I'll most definitely need the caffeine push to get me through the next couple of hours—especially when I know what, or who, is waiting on the other side.

"Hi," I say when Brian opens his front door, an unexpected wave of jitters rolling through me.

"Hey." He gives me a warm smile, and we spend a charged moment just staring at each other, like neither of us are quite sure how to act now that there aren't any restrictions or barriers to the pull we feel toward each other. I don't normally feel flustered, especially around guys, so this is new to me.

Clearing my throat, I walk past him when he opens the door to invite me in, trying my best to mentally shake it off. The inside of his bungalow looks just as I remember from the last time I was here a few months ago with John. It's cozy and warm, the kitchen on the left neatly organized, the living room on the right a mix of coastal blues and neutrals layered together, every pillow and blanket in its place. It's all exactly the same as before, but it feels different this time.

It feels like Brian.

Like I know a part of him on another level now, so now my eyes are seeing everything differently.

"What do you want to do this afternoon?" he asks from behind me, moving into the kitchen. I lean over until my forearms rest on top of the island, facing him as he leans back against the counter, crossing his arms in a way that makes his tattoos jump when he inadvertently flexes.

"Doesn't matter to me. You pick."

"Let's go for a walk on the beach," he suggests, bringing his eyes to mine. "There are a couple random hills and trails just down the coastline a little way. What do you think?"

"I'm in," I say happily, clapping my hand on the island before straightening to stand. I wonder if he realizes that he could literally throw out any suggestion right now, and I'd be up for it. There's not a lot that I would say no to.

"Let's do it."

"Want a water for the road?" he asks, reaching into his fridge, waving a bottle at me.

"Sure. Thanks." He hands it gently to me when we meet at the end of the island. He places his hand on the small of my back, guiding me toward the door, and I can't help but zero in on the warmth that his touch leaves on my skin. He pulls the door closed behind him, and we head down the porch steps right onto the beach.

"Do you need to stretch before we go? Loosen the muscles up?" I tease as I slide my sunglasses on.

"Ha. Ha. Very funny. I didn't realize that you considered twenty-six old."

I lift my shoulders and flash him a smug smile. "It is when I'm twenty-four."

He shakes his head ever so slightly, and I laugh, wrapping my hand around the crook of his arm where his elbow meets his upper arm. "I'm just kidding."

He chuckles, steering me to the left, just past a cluster of palm trees where it opens up to a stretch of open sand, the rolling ocean on our right. "I know…although, sometimes I do feel like an old man."

"Oh, whatever," I laugh, "you're in, like, perfect shape."

His bottom lip pushes out in a confident smirk. "Thank you for noticing."

I roll my eyes behind my sunglasses but secretly grin on the inside. We walk closer to the shore, and I take my hands from Brian's arm so I can slip my tennis shoes off to let the ocean wash over my feet.

"This is really pretty over here," I say as we follow the curve of the shoreline to where it turns into a mix of grass and rock. A small U-shaped cove forms around a stretch of sand.

"I actually own this," he says so quietly I can barely hear him over the crashing of a wave onto the shore.

"You what?" I rack my brain, trying to remember if this is information I would have known already or not. He peers at me, then dips his head in a nod.

"I own these five acres next to my house." He runs his hand through his thick hair, messing up a couple sections on the very top. "When I was looking for a house to buy, my realtor mentioned that this lot was about to be listed as well at a crazy low price. Apparently, the owner was pricing it low, so it would move fast. He wanted to wash his hands of it and move to the Big Island. I ended up buying the bungalow as well as this land before it even hit the market."

"Wow, I had no idea."

"Didn't really share it with a lot of people." He shrugs, kicking a random rock out of the way.

"What do you plan to do with it?"

"I'm not sure. It would be a good spot to build a house someday. Or I might not do anything with it and leave it as is. It's kind of nice just knowing this is mine, and no one else can build on it, you know? I like not having any neighbors on this side. It's quiet." He smiles.

"This is really cool, Brian." I look behind me, taking in the full land that he owns. "I doubt that owning land is in the cards for me, but I love this for you. Very impressive—and it's beautiful."

"Why is it not in the cards for you?"

"If you haven't noticed, I don't like being in one place for too long. I don't like feeling tied down to one particular place— wouldn't really make sense to own something. But never say never." I flash him a smile which he responds to with a nod and smile of his own, but I don't miss how his eyes stay on me for an extra beat.

"Here, this way. There's a little trail up here over the hill," he says.

He leads me up to a small bushy hill, stopping right at the beginning of the incline to reach back and hold out his hand.

"Coming?"

15

BRIAN

She slides her fingers between mine and trails behind me as I lead her up the hill and onto a walking path that takes us off my property and onto state land.

"So, how's the whole photography thing going? Still enjoying it?" I ask, the trail widening enough that I slow to let her catch up beside me. I keep a strong grip on her hand, though —I like the way her hand feels in mine.

"I really am," she says, her whole face lighting up. "I was up way too late last night editing images of the lighthouse. I just couldn't stop…. There's just something about starting with a regular old object and then knowing that there are so many different ways that you can tell its story. Different angles, different lighting, different focus, different background. Each one has the ability to completely change what you want the picture to say, you know? How you want it to feel. What emotions you want to evoke from the person looking at it." She pauses briefly. "Sorry, I'm rambling. It's just crazy to me that I never fully appreciated this before."

"You don't have to apologize. It just shows that you're passionate about it. It means something to you. That's great." I smile at her.

"So, do you think you'll try and do something full-time with it? Or just do it as a hobby?"

"I'm not sure. I need to figure out what my next steps are first. My plan was never to stay home here this long. I'll be moving somewhere else eventually," she says confidently, and even though I've always known that she didn't want to stay, her words still cause a small wave of disappointment to run through me. It's not that I have unrealistic expectations about our situation. Girls like Quinn don't settle down. I know that. I know whatever this is is casual, but I still don't want to think about when she might actually leave. That detail is out of sight, out of mind, as far as I'm concerned.

I nod in response, wanting to be supportive. "Have you figured out what kind of photography you enjoy the most?"

"I think landscape is my favorite. I still need to play around a little more with lifestyle shots, though. Maybe I'll ask Paige if she wants some family pictures taken on the beach."

I guide her to take a sharp right, narrowly avoiding a large boulder that borders the trail.

"So, that fishing tournament sounds exciting," she says. "Do you do it every year?"

"Pretty much. Last year we came in third. That's the highest I've ever ranked. It would be awesome to place even higher one of these years."

"What would you do with the money if you win?"

"I dunno." I sigh, feeling the urge to open up. "Honestly, I would love to use the prize money to add another boat to the business. It'd be a great way to expand, and then Ethan would have his own boat to captain."

I feel her eyes roaming over me before she says cautiously, "Is that a goal you have for your business? Or would you be doing that to benefit your brother?"

I smirk, wondering how she can cut through the bullshit and see directly into my mind. Into me.

"Probably both," I admit. "I don't necessarily need to expand, but why not? Especially if it helps him out, too, in the long run."

She swings our connected hands playfully. "I think you're the most selfless person I've ever met."

"Stop." I laugh at her playfulness.

"I'm serious." She huffs a laugh as well. "You're a good man, Brian Sanderson."

I shake my head, brushing her statement off. I don't need a lot of validation in my life—never have—but I like the fact that she thinks of me in a positive way.

We walk forward a few steps until she suddenly stops and inhales a small gasp. Her face completely drains of color, eyes darting around like she's suddenly confused. I look around, attempting to find whatever it is she's looking at, but I only find palm trees, brush, the walking trail, and the ocean in the distance. Nothing out of the ordinary.

"What is it?" I ask her.

"I've been here," she says quietly, remembering something. "My dad took us on this trail when I was around ten."

My heart beats a little faster. I stay quiet, letting her say as much as she wants to, fully aware of the fact that she's mentioning her dad and not shutting down. After a moment, she continues, her eyes glazed over, lost somewhere deep in the memory.

"It was on a Sunday," she says slowly. "I remember because that's the day Mom had her garden club meetings. Every Sunday afternoon, she would head for town, and Dad would take John and me somewhere new. A new park, new hiking trail, new food truck on the beach. Didn't matter as long as whatever we did was something we hadn't done before. Sunday Afternoon Escapades, he would call it." She nods at the trail. "This is one of the trails he took us to. No clue how he found it, but he took us here one Sunday. He loved finding stuff off the beaten path like this—places that weren't tourist-ridden."

It's quiet for a minute, and when I'm pretty sure she's done, I take the opportunity to see if she'll say more.

"Do you think that's where you get your love of adventure from?" I ask as gently as possible, fully aware of the magnitude of this moment. She blinks a few times, then her face becomes less cloudy, eventually snapping out of the trance she was in and morphing into a completely different facade.

I can visually see her process of shutting down. Moving the memory to the side. I watch as she takes a deep breath in and out, coming back to her old self, moving on as if my question to her didn't still hang in the air.

"You know what I remember?" She peers at me, excitement building in her smile.

"What's that?" I say slowly, having no idea what she's about to say.

"Come on." She pulls on my hand as she rushes up the trail. "It's right up here."

I laugh as she pulls harder, increasing her pace, practically skipping down the slight decline of the hill. The path veers to the left, but Quinn takes a right, choosing a trail that looks like it might have maybe been well traveled once but not in ages. We come up to a large dome-shaped rock nestled close to shore.

"Where are we going?" I ask, confused.

"If I remember correctly…there should be an entrance right over…here!" She pulls back some brush to reveal an opening down into a dark cavern of some sort. She sets her shoes on the ground and then places her hands on both sides of the opening, positioning herself like she's about to climb in.

"You're going in there?" I ask in surprise. She looks back at me with a grin, her dark eyes pinning me with a dare.

"Come on, Brian. Live a little!" She drops, disappearing all the way into the cavern with one jump. Curiosity gets the best of me, and I follow, peering into the opening. I can't see much from here, so I slip my shoes off and slide down, my feet hitting the sandy bottom.

It's a small cove, the walls entirely made of lava rock. There's a large opening on the far side where small waves from the ocean roll inside, over the sandy floor, coming to a stop about halfway in before receding back out. It's damp and dark in this corner, but light from the sun pours in with the waves, creating a sweeping, fading strip of light that becomes nearly nonexistent by the time it reaches us near the back. Quinn's making small circles, slowly taking it all in.

"Isn't it amazing?" she breathes, the slight echo from her voice vibrating throughout the whole cove. I find it hard to move my gaze from the look of complete exhilaration on her face. Her eyes are lit up in a way that I've discovered are only like that when she's fully lost in the world around her. It makes the small part of me that houses spontaneous energy buzz a little bit stronger, some of her excitement clearly rubbing off on me.

"I had no idea this existed," I breathe.

"I don't think many people do," she muses, running her hand along the hard wall. I walk toward the opening, stepping into the wave of water that flows in, and I peer out. I see the beach a little ways off to the right, solid rock to the left, but straight ahead is all ocean.

"I love coming across random hidden gems like this. Just like my dad," she says quietly from the far end. The emotion in her voice makes me turn toward her, my eyes taking a second to re-adjust to the dark. My legs instantly move me toward her without hesitation. By the time I reach her, her face is soft, but there's also a hint of pain under the surface. I lean my shoulder against the rock next to her, angling myself in.

"I don't normally talk about them," she whispers, looking down at her feet.

"I know," I respond just as quietly.

"I mean, really. I don't talk about them. Period."

"I got that sense," I say with a nod, not really sure what else to say.

She keeps her head down but peers over at me. "I don't know why it's a little easier with you."

A warmth spreads through my chest at her comment. I'm glad she feels comfortable with me. "Maybe it's because you know you can trust me. That I'll listen."

She nods, spending a moment in silence, then her mouth lifts up into a soft smile. "So, apparently, everyone we know knows about us now. John's worried I'm going to trample all over your poor little heart." She smirks.

"Hey, I'm a willing participant in whatever this is. Don't worry about me." I grin slowly at her, our eyes connecting and holding. The air between us sparks, and this time, I don't fight the constant pull to be closer to her.

"We're having fun, right?" she says, pulling me in with her stare that's all of a sudden tinged with a dare. I keep inching closer until I'm standing directly in front of her.

"Having a lot of fun." My voice comes out low and barely above a whisper, not even with enough force to warrant an echo. She bites the corner of her lip and slides her hands slowly up the length of my arms until they rest behind my neck, sending a shiver down my spine. I bring a hand up to gently grip her waist.

The smirk that's tugging at the corner of my mouth grows wider as I slowly dip my head, pausing just before I reach hers. I flick my eyes up to lock with hers briefly, then proceed to bring my lips to hers.

I bring one arm up to cradle the back of her head and slide

the other hand around until it's resting on her lower back, fingers splayed on the top curve of her butt. I push into her, careful to make sure my arms are the only part of either of us pressing into the rock behind her. We kiss in the dark corner of the cove, the sound of water sweeping across the sand behind us, thoroughly lost in each other.

After a few minutes, I reluctantly loosen my grip, separating from her, but still hover over her, her hands still around my neck. When I open my eyes, they register the heat behind hers for a brief second before she gently pulls my neck lower for another kiss. My heart is beating wildly in my chest as she squeezes herself closer to me, the faint sound of water drops echoing around us. I run my hands up the span of her back, bringing them slowly toward her sides until they rest along her ribcage. When she eventually pulls away, I slide my hands slowly down the side of her body, coming to a stop at her hips.

"Now, how do we get out of here?"

16

QUINN

My hands curl and pull the comforter up over the bottom half of my face. I'm wide awake and have been for a while, but I don't feel like getting up yet. A melancholy that sits heavy in my bones is ruminating inside me, making it hard to muster the energy to crawl out of bed. I didn't have a dream about my parents, but for whatever reason, they were on my mind from the second I opened my eyes. Sometimes their presence and memories come on suddenly and so overwhelmingly that it's hard to ignore. Oftentimes, it's more exhausting to fight it, so I sit in it a while, even though it hurts. God, I miss them so much.

I'm still surprised that I was able to mention them to Brian yesterday. It's not that I avoid my grief, but it's very much been a solitary journey for me. I don't share it with anyone. With the exception of the grief counselor that my aunt insisted I see for two years after they died, I haven't talked about it with anyone else. It's something that exists in my heart and my mind, and talking about it out loud seems so overwhelming and heavy—so unnatural. Like standing at the very tip of a slippery slope. Verbalizing the words makes me feel like I might slip off the edge into a never-ending, crushing snowball effect of anger, sadness, and desperation that I might never get out of.

So, I just don't talk about them out loud. Not even with John. We grieved in our own ways, and then he was even more closed off when he was struggling with PTSD. I can admit that we don't exactly have a strong history of opening up to each other. We're bonded in a way because of the shared experience, but in more of a quiet, understanding, not-spoken-out-loud kind of way. My friends from high school didn't know how to treat me after they died, and I often ignored their sympathies, preferring to lean on them for a distraction instead. We fell into a habit of avoiding the topic, and eventually, they stopped asking how I was doing or if I was okay. Most of those friendships have fizzled out over the years. I've lived the past several years silently carrying the grief with me, trying to put more of a focus on the brighter, more fun side of my life that doesn't feel as heavy.

I'm not sure if it's Brian's steady confidence or his calming energy, but something about him made me push through the urge I had to shut down yesterday when I remembered my dad taking us on the same trail. Maybe it was because my hand was in his, and he was grounding me to reality. Or maybe it was because I felt safe with him.

Whatever the reason, it was something that's never happened before. With anyone. I usually have a physical response to people getting too close, and when I feel the familiar swirling in my stomach, that's been my sign to pack up and hit the road. That was exactly what happened with my ex in Alaska. It was light and fun for the first several months, but when he started dropping hints about a future together, I immediately shut down, ready for my next adventure. I've been perfectly content keeping people at a safe distance, not letting anyone get too close to this part of my heart. But Brian was the first person that I've felt even a tiny inkling to open up to, even if it was in such a small way.

My phone buzzes with a text message from the nightstand on my right, pulling me out of my thoughts. I sneak my arm out of the covers and grab my phone.

Brian: My leg looks like I was in a fight with a tiger shark.

My laugh cuts through the silence as I remember our feeble attempt to exit the cove yesterday. After weighing our options, he had hoisted me up onto his shoulders to climb out of the same opening that we had come in. I managed to get out fairly easily, but when he tried to climb up the wall leading to the opening, he scraped his calf pretty good on some rocks.

Quinn: Do you need me to come over and administer more aid?

Quinn: Don't answer that. That sounded dirty.

Brian: Haha. Ignoring that comment. Whatever you did yesterday seemed to help. It'll be alright.

I had helped him hobble back to his house and used the first aid kit he kept under his kitchen sink to clean it up and bandage it.

Quinn: Send me a picture.

Brian: That comment's harder to ignore…

Quinn: Of your leg! Goodness, haha.

Brian: Just messing with you. Leg's fine. Matt asked if I'd take him and Elliot dolphin watching this morning, then I'm taking some clients out snorkeling this afternoon.

Brian: Can I call you later?

Quinn: Of course. Have fun!

I let my phone drop onto the mattress beside my pillow, feeling notably lighter than I did before. I inhale one last deep breath, stretching my arms above my head, finally feeling ready to make the most of the day. But before I can move on and get out of bed, I close my eyes, think of my parents, and whisper one last thing.

"aloha au iā 'oe mau loa.
I love you forever."

"How was dolphin watching this morning?" I ask Matt, slightly shifting his open palm that's laid out on top of the bar. I do the same to the other hand and then use my thumb and pointer finger to tilt his chin down and slightly to the right.

"Perfect." I back up until my back touches a chair and bring the camera up to my eyes.

"It was good. We saw a ton of dolphins. Elliot had a blast."

I gasp, lowering the camera. "Don't move your face!"

"You asked me a question," he says through clenched teeth.

"Shh," I quiet him. When I asked Paige if she was interested in me taking some family photos, she casually mentioned that Matt was redesigning the bar's website and might also be in need of some updated pictures.

"I still don't understand why I need to be in the picture. I thought we were just doing pictures of the bar," he grumbles, then instantly transforms his face into a picture-perfect smile that I'm sure has been well rehearsed.

"Oh, hush," I say, waving him off. "People want to see your face. Now just stand there and look pretty."

I snap a couple shots of him in various positions. A few with his arms crossed, leaning his hip against the counter, and a couple more of him seated on a barstool.

"Okay, how about you make some cocktails? I'll take some of you pouring drinks."

"How about we talk about this thing between you and Brian? That's what I'm dying to talk about," he says, scooping some ice into a glass.

"Hmmm, how about we don't?" I smile smugly behind the camera, zooming in to get a close-up of the glass.

"I mean, I'm glad it's you and not Tori," he rambles on. "I don't think I'd be quite as understanding as John is if my sister started a relationship with one of my best friends."

"It's not a relationship. It's a casual…situation," I say, finally finding the right word, "not that it's any of your business."

"A casual *situation*." He puts the last word in air quotes, then nods his head. "Mm-hmm. Heard that one before."

"How about a martini? I'll get one of you with the shaker," I tell him, putting an end to the conversation.

"Alright," he grumbles. After I take a couple of images, his cell phone dings with a text message from the corner of the bar top. He quickly glances at it.

"Ah, shoot, Lucy's sick," he says to himself before typing a response and setting his phone back down.

"Let's move outside," I suggest. "I want to get some of you in front of the sign." I'm already heading for the door, and thankfully, Matt follows without much of a fight.

"Okay, I want you to lean over the railing here, looking out at the ocean." He sighs and hunches over the railing. I adjust his posture a little bit, then take a few shots of him with the Matt's Beach Bar sign in front of him.

"Cool. I think we're done. I got some really good ones. Do you want to see?" I hold up the display screen to scroll through the images, but he waves me off.

"Nah, I trust you."

"Hey, guys!" Mia calls from behind me. When I turn around, I see her and John walking on the sand toward us.

"Hey!" I say, "I didn't know you were swinging by today."

"Mia insisted," John replies, squeezing my shoulder in greeting as he passes by.

"If you're trying to get dirt out of her on Brian, don't bother," Matt says dryly. "I already tried."

"Aw, really?" Mia pouts. "I just want to know how things are going. Good? Are you in love?"

I can't help the laugh that bursts out of me as I shake my head.

"Cause he's a total babe," she continues, her eyes widening as if to really drive the point home.

"Mia," John says with disgust, looking entirely uncomfortable. He runs his hand through his hair before looking my way. "Like I said, I won't stand in your way," he says to me. "I'm just gonna need a little time to get used to it, okay?"

"Noted." I nod my head, completely understanding and respecting his point of view. Matt heads back inside the building, and the rest of us trail behind.

"Did he make the first move, or did you?" Mia whispers from behind my shoulder.

"Mia! Stop, please," John laughs, throwing his arm around her shoulders, pulling her in to give her a kiss on the top of her head.

"Don't worry, I have no interest in talking about it," I say with a smile, returning my camera to its case. Matt walks back behind the bar while John and Mia slide onto some barstools.

"Hey, you said Lucy's sick, right? I don't have any plans right now. I can fill in if you're short-handed." I offer to Matt.

"That would be great, actually. Thanks, Quinn," Matt says.

"No problem. Be back in a few." I take the bag and my purse toward the back room to shift into server mode for the evening.

17

———

QUINN

"Now, this is my kind of casual date," I say excitedly as Brian parks his truck in a small parking lot on the outer edge of the Honolulu International Airport. The lot is connected to a tarmac where an open-door helicopter sits.

"I figured you'd like it." He laughs, shifting the gear into park. "Chuck, the pilot, owes me a favor. He does private helicopter tours, and a little while back, he somehow overbooked himself and called me super last minute, begging me to entertain one of the groups with a fishing charter."

"Which, of course, you did," I point out the obvious while settling my sling purse across my shoulder, cross-body style, and grabbing my camera out of its case.

"I did. He offered me a flight anytime I wanted one." He smiles at me, unbuckling his seat belt. "Haven't wanted one 'till now."

"Well, I am one lucky lady," I say, leaning over to give him a kiss on the cheek before climbing out of the truck.

"Eeek!" I yip, hardly able to contain my excitement as I skip around the back of the truck to connect with Brian. I slide my hand in his and grab the same wrist with my other hand, shaking it back and forth.

"I'm so excited! I've never been in an open-door one before, have you?" I ask.

"I haven't. I'm excited, too. I thought maybe it'd be easier to take pictures, too, since you're not looking through glass."

"Absolutely. Thanks for telling me to bring my camera." I smile up at him just as a man comes walking out of the helicopter hangar. He has a laid-back style about him, with a faded button-down shirt to go with his jeans and scruffy facial hair.

"Brian. My man," he says, giving him a firm handshake.

"Chuck." Brian nods in greeting. "This is Quinn."

"Quinn, pleasure to meet you," he says to me before turning his attention back to Brian.

"I'm glad you're finally taking me up on my offer. I don't like having unfulfilled debts," he chuckles. "I've been harping on you forever to come flying. I'm guessing this lovely lady here is the reason you changed your mind?"

"She is," he says with subtle conviction and a curt nod that causes my stomach to dip. Chuck looks between us with a knowing smile, then turns toward the helicopter.

"So, I'm planning to take you up for about an hour. We'll go all around Oahu. Brian mentioned you're a photographer, so I'll make sure to get you nice and close. There are some amazing views from up there."

I nod my head in agreement, but I'm stuck on the fact that Brian called me a photographer. No one has ever called me that before, and I like the sound of it.

"Sounds great," Brian says.

"Let's go!" Chuck leads us closer to the helicopter and motions for us to climb inside. Excitement starts buzzing as I settle in a seat, the open doorway on my left. Brian slides in next to me, with the open side on his right. I squeal as we get buckled, and Chuck hands us each a headset. I slide mine on, adjusting the mouthpiece. After swinging the camera strap over my neck, I grip both hands around Brian's bicep and squeal, my thumb grazing across the ink that's sealed on his skin.

"Alright, here we go, guys!" Chuck says through the headset as the blades start turning, slowly at first, then increasing rapidly. He makes some communication with air traffic control, and soon enough, we're lifting into the air. I don't even attempt to hide the smile that's taken up my entire face as we get higher, the airport getting smaller below. A rush runs through me, and I relish every single second of it.

I let go of Brian's arm and grip my camera, ready to start shooting. Brian scoots himself a little lower in his seat, getting comfortable, and rests his left hand on my thigh by my knee, settling his fingers in the gap between my legs. I look at him out of the corner of my eye, but he's calmly looking past me out my side of the helicopter. He glances at me and smiles warmly, a gleam in his eye like just maybe he's enjoying this, too.

Chuck takes us along the coast and past Diamond Head, a massive volcanic cone, one of Oahu's most recognized landmarks, and I immediately snap several pictures. The hint of a rainbow peeks through a cloud, disappearing behind the rim of the large crater, creating the most incredible image. When Chuck moves along, I tilt the camera to show Brian one of the images, and he gives me a thumbs up, his eyebrows raising like he's impressed. Adrenaline rushes through me as we lift higher and tilt slightly to the right, causing me to lean into Brian's side.

"Ahh!" I laugh, wrapping my arms around his forearm that's still gripping my leg. He grins back at me, giving me a close-up view of his dimple, his hand squeezing my leg. We continue on, passing Hanauma Bay, the Makapu'u lighthouse and Lanikai Beach. All the while, I obsessively take photo after photo, each angle and image too good to pass by. The crystal-blue water at Kaneohe Bay looks particularly majestic from this high up, and I focus on the offshore sandbar that's settled in the middle of the bay.

The loud thumping of the helicopter blades, plus the exhilaration of there being no barrier between me and the sky, mixed with the sight of the island eight hundred or so feet below us…all of it is adding to the absolute euphoria that's bubbling in my chest.

"Having fun?" Brian asks into the headset, studying me, then chuckling when I nod vigorously. Chuck takes us over a few other scenic destinations, notably the Dole Plantation and Pearl Harbor, before arriving back at the airport.

I'm disappointed that our helicopter ride is coming to an end, but I'm also still giddy to have experienced such a thrilling experience with Brian at all. Once we land and he gives us the okay, I take a deep breath before unbuckling my seatbelt, removing the headset and hopping out. My legs feel wobbly, like they need a little time to distribute the adrenaline and charged energy that's been buzzing for the last hour.

"Thank you so much, Chuck," Brian says, shaking his hand.

"Yes, thank you!" I throw my arms around Chuck in a hug. "That was so amazing!"

"My pleasure. Got a little rocky up there with some turbulence, but you guys handled it like champs."

"Let me know if you ever need anything else, Chuck. Thanks again," Brian says before grabbing my hand and walking back toward his truck.

"Oh my gosh, that was incredible," I gush, taking another deep breath, wanting to savor the high still running through me.

"It really was," he agrees, leading me to the passenger side and opening the door for me.

"Thank you, sir."

"I'm not sure how you'll ever top this date," I tease when he slides into the driver's seat.

"Date's not over yet," his voice comes out low and steady, which makes me aware of my heartbeat all of a sudden. Instead of taking a right out of the parking lot, he turns left onto a grassy hill on the outskirts of the airport.

"Where are we going?" I laugh.

"You'll see." He circles the truck, so it's facing the highway. Reaching over, he turns the volume up on the radio, which is playing "Tequila Sunrise" by The Eagles.

"Come on," he tells me, getting out of the truck. Thoroughly confused, I get out and meet Brian at the back, where he's pulling down the tailgate. He grabs a blanket from the back seat and lays it out gently before patting it.

"Sit," he says. "I'll be right back."

"You're leaving?" I ask in disbelief once I pull myself up to sit. A smirk pulls at the corner of his mouth, eyes piercing mine. He comes to stand between my legs, gently spreading them wider, coming as close as the truck will allow. His head angles slowly toward mine, making my breath catch in my chest.

"Trust me," he whispers, then gives me a quick kiss on the lips before backing away and walking briskly down the hill.

"What in the world," I whisper to myself as I watch him go, wondering where on earth he's going. For about twenty minutes, I swing my dangling legs, watching cars pull in and out of the airport parking lot, until eventually, I see Brian walking back with a pineapple in each hand, straws sticking out of the tops.

I gasp and grin at him. "Are those pineapple coladas?" The inside is hollowed out and filled to the top with piña colada, one of my favorite drinks. I wonder if he knows that.

"Yup." He hands me one and then uses his one free hand to hoist himself up to sit next to me. "There are a couple food trucks set up along the road right outside the parking lot. We're gonna sit here, listen to some good music, drink these enormous pineapples"—he points to the runway just beyond the helicopter hangar—"and watch airplanes take off."

My smile forms over the straw that's already in my mouth. "I love that," I say, taking another sip.

"The helicopter ride was pretty cool, huh?" he asks.

"Brian, it was perfect, honestly. I loved every single second." I set the pineapple down next to me. "The adrenaline rush never gets old. Gosh, I live for doing things like that. Things that bring you to the brink of your limits, forcing you to throw inhibition to the wind, laughing in fear's face. Stuff like that feeds my soul."

He leans back on one straightened-out arm behind him and smiles at me. "I'm glad you enjoyed it. That was my goal."

Just then, an airplane takes off on the stretch of runway in front of us, lifting up to ascend into the air.

"Where do you think that one's heading?" he asks, his gaze focused on the plane that's getting smaller in the sky.

"Hmm, good question…my guess is Utah," I say the first random state that comes to mind.

"I'll say Texas."

"Where would you want to travel to if you could?" I ask him, remembering our conversation about him not having traveled anywhere.

He shrugs, looking deep in thought. "Probably try to go to Cali. I've heard Santa Cruz and Huntington Beach are great surfing spots."

I nod as we watch another plane take off.

"That one's going to Chicago," I comment.

"Nah"— he shakes his head—"definitely Arizona."

I laugh, taking another sip, and then I elbow him.

"Hey, thank you for today," I say softly. He smiles at me, then his eyes drop to my lips. A spark trickles up my spine as he slowly leans in to kiss me, bringing his free hand to cradle my jaw. His thumb grazes my cheek, and then he breaks the kiss with a smile.

"You're welcome," he says quietly, going back to his pineapple, leaving me trying to catch my breath and slow down my heart rate. Then, Brian's phone buzzes with a text message. He pulls it out of his pocket and types something quickly before putting it back.

"That was my mom," he explains, "asking if I could come over and help her fix her washing machine."

"What did you say? Do we need to go?"

He peers at me, his dark eyes holding mine.

"I told her I'll come by tomorrow. Tonight I'm doing something for me."

With that, I slide closer and rest my head on his shoulder. We spend the rest of the evening sipping our pineapples, guessing where each plane is heading, and I find myself thinking this is, hands down, the best date I've ever been on.

18

BRIAN

Switching back to the local classic rock station on my truck's radio, I pull out of my driveway and head for my mom's house. As I drive, my mind wanders to my date with Quinn yesterday. The way she squealed with excitement when the helicopter made a turn…the look on her face when she was scrolling through the pictures she had just taken…the look on her face after I kissed her. As much as I'm trying to manage my expectations and be realistic about where she stands on relationships, I'm having a hard time dialing in my feelings for her.

I can hardly get a handle on how hard my chest is pounding right now just thinking about her, and it beats ten times faster when I'm actually with her. When she's near me, I don't want to leave her, and when I'm not with her, she's all I can think about. As much as it sucks, I know her stance, so I'll do my best to keep it as casual as I can and follow her lead. Man, go figure. If someone would have told me a month ago that I would be falling for John's sister—a girl I've only ever seen as a friend—I'd have laughed in their face. I definitely did not see this, or her, coming. I pull into Mom's driveway and head in through the front door, knocking as I open it.

"Hello," I call out, but no one answers. I head to the laundry room and hear muffled voices as I get closer.

"Here, try this one," Mom says, bent down, holding out a pair of pliers to Ethan, who's on his side on the floor, his hands stretched behind the washing machine. I fold my arms in amusement and lean against the door frame to see how this is going to play out. As far as I know, Ethan's never even picked up a tool in his life—not that I've ever witnessed, anyway.

"I don't need that one," Ethan grumbles, dismissing her with a wave of his hand. A clinkering sound comes from behind the machine where he's working.

"I mean, maybe we should wait for Brian to get here. He said he was on his way," Mom mutters.

"Just give me a second," Ethan grumbles. I watch, fighting the urge to jump in and make sure he isn't making it worse back there. Mom straightens and notices me out of the corner of her eye.

"Brian! I didn't hear you come in."

"Just got here," I reply, focusing on Ethan. "Do you know what you're doing back there?"

"You guys have no faith in me," he says flatly but continues nonetheless.

"I've just never seen you try and fix something before," I tell him. "It's kind of freaking me out."

"Yeah, well, you weren't here… Somebody had to fix it." He climbs up off of the floor, picking up the tools that are splayed out.

"There. Go ahead and inspect it," he says to me, moving to the side. "You know you want to."

I crouch down and take a look, wiggling a few things and

making sure certain screws are tight. To my surprise, everything looks exactly how it should.

"I think you actually fixed it," I say in surprise, coming back up to stand.

"Ethan! Thank you," Mom says, throwing her arms around him in a hug. He scowls, looking uncomfortable in her arms, but I don't miss the small trace of pride on his face.

"Well, I guess I wasn't needed after all, was I?" I say.

"I guess not. I appreciate you coming, though," Mom says to me, squeezing my arm.

"No prob. I'll talk to you later, then. I have some errands to run," I say, giving her a quick hug. "Ethan, don't get a big head and start taking everything apart around here, okay?"

He doesn't bother to respond, but I can practically feel the eye roll from behind me as I walk away.

"I brought take-out," Quinn says brightly with a grin when I open my door. She's wearing a black T-shirt with white cut-off jean shorts and huge, tortoise-shaped sunglasses that overpower the frame of her face. A ray of bright sunshine gleams behind her, framing her in a golden light. I don't think I've ever seen a sight more beautiful.

"Hi," I respond with a smile of my own, taking the food from her and kissing her on the forehead. She wraps her arms around my middle, fisting my gray sweatshirt at my lower back, hanging on like maybe she just needs something to cling to for a minute. I wrap my free hand around her, under the back of her head, giving her the best one-handed hug I can manage.

"I will say, the free food is one definite perk of working at Matt's." She releases me and makes her way inside, setting her bags on the kitchen table that never gets used. "I even swiped an extra salsa container for later." The look of pride on her face makes me chuckle.

I slide my loose pile of budget spreadsheets and expense reports that I was initially planning to go through tonight to the side and grab two plates from the cabinet before opening the bag. *The Very Best of The Rolling Stones* is softly playing from the vinyl player in the corner of the living room next to the TV, creating a soft, comfortable ambiance for us.

I place two heaping shrimp tacos on a plate, spread out some chips, and add a container of salsa next to them before sliding it to where she's sitting on a barstool.

"Something to drink? I can't whip up a pineapple colada— I'm not that fancy—but I have beer."

She laughs, popping a chip in her mouth. "Beer's great, thanks."

I grab two beers from the fridge and place one in front of her, then make a plate of my own.

"I'm out of paper towels. I'm gonna grab some from the closet. Be right back," I say, making my way down the hall to the little supply closet on the left.

"Okay," she says cheerfully, taking a bite of the taco. By the time I make it back, she's already finished one whole taco and is starting in on the second.

"These look delicious," I say, sliding onto the barstool next to her.

"They are." She nods. "So, how was your day?"

"Pretty good. Worked this morning and then stopped by my mom's house."

"Were you able to fix her washing machine?"

"Actually, Ethan fixed it. He was already working on it by the time I got there, which is actually a big deal. He doesn't voluntarily offer to help with anything, especially when he knows I'm on the way."

Her eyebrows lift as she takes a sip of her beer. "That's a good thing, right?"

"It's a step in the right direction, that's for sure."

With a nod, she resumes eating. When we're both finished, I grab both of our plates to bring to the sink.

"Oh! I want to show you what I was working on this morning," she says, retrieving her laptop out of her bag and bringing it back to the island. I rinse my hands and come around the back of her stool, leaning in to place a hand on either side of the counter, caging her in as she powers it on, and we wait for her editing software to load. I can't resist inching my face even closer, moving her hair to the side with my chin, then bringing my lips to the spot where the top of her shoulder meets her neck.

"Hmm," she hums, settling back farther into the cocoon I created around her. I place another kiss a little higher, right behind her jaw, under her ear. I can feel the shiver on my lips as it runs across her skin, and I smile against her neck.

"Brian," she whispers.

"Mmm," I murmur, making my way back down the column of her neck.

"Are you trying to distract me?"

"Uh-uh." I shake my head but don't stop what I'm doing.

"Okay, here," she says, clearing her throat, shifting slightly forward. I grin, liking the fact that I make her flustered, and settle my chin on her shoulder, focusing on the laptop screen.

"I edited a few of these this morning. Look how stunning." She opens an image she took from our helicopter ride of Diamond Head with the rainbow in the background and enlarges it.

"Wow. Quinn, that's really incredible," I tell her, meaning every word. The colors, the angle, all the little details—it's very impressive.

"You think so?"

"Absolutely. I'd hang that on my wall," I say, to which she laughs. "Show me another one."

She opens the next five images, each one just as stunning as the last.

"I'll show you more when I finish editing them," she says as she closes the laptop. And that's when I notice it.

The glass jar.

Sitting on the counter next to the tray where I throw my keys.

"Quinn," I say softly.

"Yeah?"

"What is this?" I push my arms off the island and walk around it to pick up the jar. Glued to the front of the jar is a piece of paper that says Brian's Travel Fund. I turn to lock eyes with Quinn, who's grinning.

"It's your travel fund." She slides off of the stool and comes to me, wrapping her arms around my middle. "I put it there when you were getting the paper towels." She smiles. "Figured it was about time you replaced the one from when you were a kid. I even started you off." She motions to the two quarters at the very bottom of the jar.

The grin that grows on my face matches the swelling in my chest as I squeeze my arm tightly around her, struggling to find the right words.

"I think that's the sweetest thing anyone's done for me," I tell her, placing the jar back on the counter and bringing both of my hands to her face, tilting it up to kiss her gently on the lips. I kiss her softly, then deeply, emotion running through me. She clings to me just as tightly, matching my energy with the kiss.

"Thank you," I whisper, looking deep into her eyes, hoping she can see my gratitude. She smiles and rests the side of her head on my chest. I place my chin gently on the top of her head, and we stay locked in the hug, neither one of us making an attempt to move. Outside the window, I can see that the sun is starting to set on the horizon above the ocean.

"You wanna go watch the sunset?" I ask. She nods against my chest. I pull my sweatshirt up and over my head before lacing my fingers through hers as I lead her out the front door. She starts heading down the porch steps, but I stop her.

"Not from the beach. This way," I tell her, bringing her to the left side of the house where the hammock sits, and I spread it open.

"Hop in."

19

QUINN

"It's so pretty," I murmur. I'm tucked up close to Brian's side under his arm that wraps around me, my head resting on his chest, the force from the hammock pushing us together. My leg is curled over his right knee, with my foot resting between his calves. The hammock is positioned so we don't even have to shift our necks or crane our heads at all to see the ocean. Resting my head against him, I have the perfect view of the beach, with a swaying palm tree branch lazily gliding in and out of view. Shades of pink and orange sweep across where the ocean meets the sky, and I desperately wish I had my camera with me.

Silence hangs in the air in a comfortable kind of way as we watch the waves crash onto shore, birds swirling in the air above. As much as I keep trying to convince myself that this thing with Brian is still just casual, the way I feel lying here, completely melded to him, is making me feel like it's turning into something more. That thought alone makes my throat want to close, and I have a strong urge to hop right out of this hammock and run far away, but there's also a small part of me that wants to stay and let him in, which is unfamiliar. I don't know this part of me—don't know if I can trust it.

I run my fingers slowly along Brian's other forearm that's resting across his stomach. I trace the outline of a cluster of small flowers that are nestled seamlessly in the middle of his sleeve of tattoos. My chest tightens, a rush of dread prickling across my skin at the memory that just popped into my head. Habit and instinct are telling me to push it back down, but that small part of me that I latch onto wonders what would happen if I just push through.

"This was my mom's favorite flower," I whisper. "A hibiscus." I pause, taking stock of how it feels to say that out loud. Brian's hand that's resting on my hip starts sliding back and forth softly, his silent way of letting me know he's listening.

"We had a couple of hibiscus shrubs that lined the front of our house, and I swear they were her prized possession." A small huff comes out, sounding partly like a laugh, partly like a strangled exhale. "Mom would spend hours pruning or trimming those things." I swallow down the lump in my throat before the words continue to pour out of me.

"For the formal school dance in eighth grade, she clipped a few and handmade me a wrist corsage to wear. She insisted the yellow flower went perfectly with my red dress. And it did."

The hand that was on my waist bends up until he's softly running his fingers through my hair, pulling it back behind my ear before coming back and doing it again. Over and over, combing through my hair, he just lets me be. And we lie there, our breathing becoming in sync, slightly bobbing as the hammock dips a little with every move of his hand through my hair.

The sky slowly starts getting darker around us. As okay as that felt to share with him, it was followed by a sharp rush of anxiety over what would happen if I shared too much—if I kept going. I take a deep breath, focusing back on the calm feeling that I felt before, letting that sweep through me until the anxiety dissipates. I lift my head, shifting so that I can lay my chin on the back of my hand on his chest, looking up at him.

"Tell me something I don't already know about you," I whisper, allowing the current of energy between us to get stronger as my eyes roam over his profile. His dark eyes look out at the coastline, squinting slightly, then he peers at me.

"Something you don't know about me?"

"Yup," I confirm with a nod. "I already know big things, like who your family and friends are. Your job. And some little things…"

"What little things?" he interrupts.

"Let's see…like the fact that you, John, and Matt went cliff diving at Spitting Caves when you were fifteen, even though my parents told you not to. That you got your first tattoo on your eighteenth birthday." He flicks his eyes to me, darkening as I continue softly. "That when we all go out to eat, you always get the mahi-mahi if it's on the menu. Stuff like that. What don't I know yet?"

He licks his lips, seemingly contemplating what he's willing to share. The corner of his mouth tilts up in the slightest way, and I can tell he's trying to tamper down a smile.

"Tell me," I laugh. "What is it?" His smile breaks out into a full-on grin.

"I don't think you're ready for this one."

"Oh, please tell me," I plead. He clears his throat before continuing.

"One of my favorite shows is *The Golden Girls*."

"Stop." I bury my head in his shirt in an attempt to not laugh out loud. "There's no way."

"It's true." He nods, and I'm impressed that even when he's

admitting to something as embarrassing as this, there's still such a confidence in his voice.

"I don't have a lot of time to watch TV in general, but at night, before I fall asleep, that's what I'll turn on. They're just so damn cute. I think Sophia's my favorite—Dorothy's mom."

This time, I can't help the giggles as they pour out of me.

"Have you seen it?" he asks, letting out a laugh of his own at the sheer ridiculousness of this conversation.

"I can't say that I have…but maybe I'll watch it sometime with you if you like it that much."

His expression softens, and he gives me a lazy smile while running his fingertips down my spine.

"Anything I don't know about you? That you want to share?" His eyes hold mine, and I can feel my heart skip a beat in my chest. It takes everything in me to not slide up and kiss him right now.

"Hmm. My favorite color is green… I despise sushi, and I collect a piece of jewelry from every place I travel to. Kind of like a souvenir." I hold up my hand where two silver wishbone stacker rings are on my pointer finger. "This ring's from New Zealand."

He takes my hand and studies the ring, then encloses his hand around my fingers, bringing them to rest on his chest.

"I love that," he says softly, his eyes boring into mine. Neither of us says another word as we allow ourselves to not look away. I can't ignore the pull any longer, so I slide up until my face is hovering over his, my body resting directly on top of him, the hammock bobbing with the movement. He smirks, bringing his hands to the top of my butt. I pause to take him in, getting distracted by how gorgeous he really is. It's almost completely dark now, but the nearby windows of his house cast some light across us, so I can still see every feature on his face. Then, I lean down slowly and press my lips to his, weaving my fingers through the netting holes above his head.

His hands grip me tighter, pulling me to him, and I deepen the kiss. A low groan escapes the back of his throat, and his hands start roaming slowly up the length of my back, then back down, leaving my skin burning in his wake as he goes. I move to kiss his jaw, peppering slow kisses all the way to the top of his neck. He grips my butt and pushes himself up against me, sending a swooping wave low in my belly. His hands come back to my upper back, and I can't get enough of how his touch makes me feel. He's cautious, yet hungry at the same time. Gentle, yet dominating. I lift slightly, and the way he looks at me makes me stop in my tracks. There's always a depth to his eyes every time I look at him, but when desire is added to that mix, the intensity is almost too much.

"Let's go inside," I whisper, then crawl off of him without bothering to wait for a response. I attempt to steady myself on solid ground until he immediately grabs the backs of my thighs, lifting me up, wrapping my legs around his waist. I place my hands on each side of his neck and kiss him deeply as he holds me with one arm, using his free arm to feel for the porch railing. Somehow, he manages to get us all the way across the porch and through the front door, bumping into the couch along the way. He slows when we get to the hallway, turning to push me against the wall.

"Quinn," he says thickly, clenching his jaw like it physically pains him to stop. "Are you sure?" I attempt to catch my breath as I process what he's doing. He's giving me an out. A chance to stop if this is too much for me or if it is crossing a line. I smile because it actually does the opposite. It only solidifies the fact that I want more of him. To get lost and consumed by this connection and to keep floating in this high of being held by him.

"I'm good," I confirm with barely a nod before bringing my mouth back against him hard, to which he responds by pushing off the wall and carrying me the rest of the way to his bedroom.

20

BRIAN

The sound of a scream wakes me from my dream the next morning. It takes a split second to fully come to reality, but when I register the fact that the scream belonged to Quinn and came from my living room, I'm on my feet and immediately rushing out of my bedroom in a panic.

"Oh my gosh," Quinn breathes, leaning on the back of the couch with her hand to her chest. "You scared me." Her cheeks are red, visibly flustered, and she's struggling to catch her breath.

Ethan's sitting on the far end of the couch with his sweatshirt hood over his head and a pile of blankets in his lap, squinting his eyes at the light I just turned on. He grumbles and puts his hand over his eyes.

"Quinn? You alright?" I ask, coming behind her, my hand finding her lower back. She blows out a deep breath and nods, avoiding making eye contact with me.

"I'm fine. I just didn't know your brother was here. I was

walking by when he asked what time it was, and I swear I almost punched him in the face."

I glare at Ethan, even though I know, technically, he didn't do anything wrong. I just hate the fact that she was startled, and he's the only person present that I can aim my disapproving glare at.

"Don't worry, I'm fine, too," he grumbles sarcastically, using the back of his hand to hide a yawn, "just over here trying to sleep."

"Shut it, Ethan," I say, not able to take my eyes off Quinn, who's moving to the kitchen table where her purse and laptop bag are. It's then that I realize that it's 4:55 a.m., not even 5:00 yet, and she's fully dressed, wearing the same clothes as last night. Now that the initial fear has subsided, and I know that she's not in harm's way, disappointment replaces it and floods through me with the knowledge that she was in the process of sneaking out without saying goodbye.

"Are you leaving?" I ask her. She turns slowly as she slips her purse over her head. Her eyes search mine for a moment before she shrugs, not doing a very good job at hiding the conflicting emotions written all over her face. Guilt, exhaustion, and confusion somehow all resonate together in the way that she purses her lips together and the way her forehead creases.

I search her face for some kind of clarity when my eye momentarily catches on the small birthmark below her left eyebrow. A memory flashes, and I remember the way that I slowly ran my thumb over it and then down the side of her face last night when I leaned over to kiss her goodnight. My stomach lurches, not just from my own hurt that she didn't bother to wake me up—especially after last night—but more so for the simple fact that she's clearly not okay. Dread creeps up my spine, and I feel panic surfacing because I don't have a firm grasp on how to handle this spiraling situation—no clear idea on what the best approach is supposed to be.

"I...I have to go," she stammers quickly, rushing out the

front door. I waste no time following her out and down the porch steps, not caring in the slightest that all I have on are my boxer briefs.

"Quinn, wait." I jog and catch up to her just as she's throwing her things in the backseat of her car. "Talk to me. What's happening?"

She closes the car door and looks at me vulnerably at first, then she clears her throat and puts her hands on her hips, staring down at the sand. I know her well enough to know that she's shutting me out. Shutting down.

"I've never done this before," she says with an uncharacteristic sharpness to her voice.

"Done what?" I ask, trying to tame the desperation that's festering inside me. Her head swings back up to lock eyes with mine.

"I've always just left right away after…you know. Being with someone. I don't sleep over. I don't cuddle. I don't connect on that level," she says firmly. The pain in her voice makes it obvious that she's regretting the fact that all of those things happened last night, which is absolutely crushing to me.

"Why is that a bad thing?" I ask cautiously, still trying to make sense of her behavior.

"Because I don't let people in, Brian. I…I just don't. I can't." She shrugs her shoulders in defeat, along with a sad attempt at a forced smile that says she accepted that this is how she operates a long time ago.

"It was too much," I say quietly, not necessarily to her—maybe even more for me—as understanding dawns on me. "Last night was too much. We shouldn't have crossed that line."

Her brows scrunch together with guilt and even deeper confusion. She shakes her head slowly, looking back down. "Last night was perfect," she whispers, her voice cracking. "I just don't know how to do everything else."

I step closer and gently grab her hand. I feel conflicted

between wanting to beg her to talk to me and not wanting to force myself on her if she's not ready. "Don't overthink it, Quinn," I say softly. "It's just me. Look at me."

She vehemently shakes her head, then retracts her hand from mine.

"This…"—she waves at the air between us—"this isn't me. In any other relationship, I would have been gone already. Long gone, actually." She pinches the bridge of her nose, sighing deeply.

"I just need some time to think." She looks up at me guiltily, then she opens her driver's side door, keeping one hand on the handle.

"Quinn, please. Don't leave." Desperation spills out of me in one last-ditch attempt to get her to stay, but I stop myself before pressing further. She purses her lips together again as I notice that her eyes have a slightly pinkish hue and are starting to water.

"I'll talk to you later, okay?" she says quietly before getting in and driving off, leaving me confused, gutted, and at a complete loss for what to do next.

"Shit, man," Ethan's groggy voice says behind me. "That was rough."

I blow out a slow, uneven breath, the ache in my chest making it difficult to release a complete exhale.

"Shut up," I murmur as I walk past him into the house.

"I'm serious. I've seen a lot of girl drama in my day, but that was crazy. She freaked out because you cuddled last night? Damn, did I hear that right?"

"Drop it, Ethan," I bark at him, heading for the fridge. My mouth is all of a sudden extremely dry and in desperate need of some water.

"Some chicks…" He shakes his head. "Just crazy."

"I said drop it. You don't know what you're talking about here. And it's also none of your business," I say calmly but with enough force that he finally leaves it alone. Because it's true; he has no idea. I know Quinn isn't just blowing me off for no reason. She has a very valid reason—and one that I completely recognize and empathize with. I don't think she realizes how transparent she is, even though she tries so hard to not be.

But I see her. I see her struggling to talk about her parents, struggling with getting too close to me, with opening up too much. And what sucks is that I completely understand why. I understand why it's hard, and I hate that it is for her. I don't blame her at all that this is how she's coped. But I also see the small part of her that is allowing me in. That's sharing things with me that I'm pretty sure she's never shared with anyone else. I see the part of her that's trying. That's the part I'm determined to hold onto while I give her the space she needs to think.

"Be ready to go in twenty," I say curtly to Ethan, then head to take a shower and prep for our full-day charter, already fully aware that work won't be nearly enough of a distraction from my thoughts today.

21

QUINN

The knock on my door breaks me out of my thoughts, bringing me back to earth. I've been in a haze ever since I left Brian's yesterday morning. Thankfully, I had a shift at the coffee shop yesterday to keep me busy, but even the busyness of that couldn't shake the lingering cloud hanging over me and the awful pain in my chest that I've had ever since.

I feel terrible about what happened yesterday. Everything was great—more than great. Incredible, actually. I was so content and happy after we slept together that I didn't even think twice about falling asleep in his arms. But when I woke up in the middle of the night, panic started to set in. What was I doing? What do these feelings mean? How did I get in so deep? It became very clear, lying in the dark with his arm draped over my stomach, that this is absolutely not casual. What I feel for Brian is the exact opposite, actually. I tried to push through the anxiety that was building in my chest, but every time I was close to falling back asleep, it bubbled right back up, refusing to let me rest. By the time morning rolled around, I was a jumbled ball of anxious energy and desperately needed to get some air. Some space.

I clear my throat and shake my hands out to calm my nerves before opening the door. Brian's standing in the hallway, head looking down, one hand fidgeting with his backward hat. He has gray workout shorts on and a white shirt that fits snugly on his chest. When he brings his head up, I can see the pain behind his eyes that matches the feeling in my chest, which only adds to my feeling of dread because I know he's in over his head, too. He feels what I feel.

"Hi," I say softly.

"Hi," he replies. When he texted me an hour ago, asking if he could stop by, I couldn't stop myself from saying yes. Because while I'm still very apprehensive and have strong, conflicting emotions about us, I also know that he's the only person capable of making this ache in my chest feel better. I've been desperate just to see him.

"Come in." I open the door wider, and he sneaks past me but stops just inside, shuffling his feet, like he doesn't want to come all the way in.

"So, I know you said you needed some time to think, and I totally respect that," he starts, his voice low and thick, "but it didn't feel right to not at least check in to make sure that you are alright."

The corner of my mouth pulls up into a small, sad smile that I'm sure conveys the worsening guilt that just hit me. Of course, he would be worried about me, even though I was the one who ran out on him yesterday.

"I'm okay," I say quietly, not quite sure what to say next. We simply stare at each other for several silent, heavy seconds.

"Listen…" he says softly, "I'm gonna back off and give you

space, but I just need to get some stuff off my chest before I do that. Is that okay?"

Words aren't coming to my mind, so I only nod, nervous anticipation buzzing at what he's about to say.

"I've had some realizations." He clears his throat before continuing. "You've made it clear since we were teenagers that you don't do long-term relationships. I've always known this about you, and honestly, I've admired it for the longest time. You knew what you wanted and didn't care what anyone thought. Well, now I see things differently." He slides his hands into the pockets of his shorts, keeping his eyes steadily on me. "I think you use it as a way to keep people at a distance. To keep them at arm's length so they don't get too close. Because I think you're terrified to lose another person you love."

Tears prick at my eyes, and a lump forms in my throat, his words burning straight into my heart. Goosebumps run down my arms, and I close my eyes briefly to steady myself before he goes on.

"You're protecting yourself by not letting people all the way in. You can't get hurt if they're not close, right? And while I know that traveling and chasing adventures are absolutely part of who you are, I also think that maybe a part of you is running. Running from your past. The memories. The pain." His eyes bore into me, and the hollow ache in my chest gets heavier, leaving me feeling completely exposed and gutted at the accuracy of his words. "Or better yet...I think you're chasing something. A feeling, maybe? A place that feels like home?"

I don't bother to wipe at the tear that falls down my cheek. Brian's eyes trail the path it takes down my face, then steps closer.

"I'm not saying this to hurt you. I just want to show you that I'm already there. I know you, Quinn. Better than you think I do. On a deeper level. Whether you want to join me here or not is up to you."

"Brian…" I whisper, pleading—for him to do what, I don't know. "It's too much," I whisper. He stares back at me with a look of desperation that mirrors exactly how I feel.

"I know you're feeling this, too, Quinn. This thing between us…I can see it in your eyes. I also know that there are probably a million reasons floating around in that head of yours, trying to talk you out of this. And maybe you already have—talked yourself out of this. But on the off chance that you haven't…I'll be here when you're ready."

My face scrunches together, trying desperately to hold everything in. I don't dare open my mouth, because the sobs would absolutely barrel their way out. All I can do is look at him, tears streaming down my face. His pained expression takes me in, then he moves toward me slowly, as if he's ready to stop at any second if I ask him to. He grabs the back of my head gently and places a soft kiss at the very center of my forehead before pulling away and retreating to the door.

When he opens it, he pauses and looks at me one last time, standing straight with confidence, but his eyes show defeat and weariness. "This doesn't scare me, Quinn. It's not too much."

He says the last part slowly, as if to make sure I'm fully absorbing the weight of his words. And with the click of the door shutting, my eyes squeeze together, and I let the tears fall, feeling completely overwhelmed and overcome with emotion. His words were the truest words spoken to me in a long time. Like he was holding a mirror up that looked directly into my soul. Into the deepest part of my heart. No one's touched that part of me in a very long time.

The thing is, he's right. I don't do it on purpose, and somewhere along the way, I started making excuses to cover up why I do it…but it's true. I push people away when they start getting too close. I literally run away, sometimes halfway across the world, when everything gets to be too much. I know that the question I have to ask myself is, do I want that to change? I wipe the tears on my face and shuffle to the couch, where I settle face down on the cushions, not having the energy to stay standing anymore.

I can feel myself attempting to push the hurt and anger to the side. Every cell of my being is aching to brush this whole thing off and just leave Oahu altogether. That's what I've always done, after all. What I've trained myself to do.

But is that what I really want? Do I want to be on the run for the rest of my life? The thought of letting someone get close to my heart, pain and all, feels so crushing. But the thought of losing Brian hurts more, and the reality of that is overwhelming.

Not able to sit still any longer, I get up. An overwhelming urge runs through me as I grab my keys and head out the door. When I pull my car out of the parking lot, I have no exact destination in mind. I just know that the walls of my apartment were starting to feel suffocating, and I needed to just get out. To wander and drive aimlessly for a while. Let my heart settle.

I drive along the coastline, taking in the palm-tree-lined streets, the swarms of vacationers waiting in line at the colorful food trucks set up along the beach. There are two people carrying a paddle board into the ocean in the distance. It makes me feel anxious, like it's all too overstimulating. I need to get away from the noise.

I drive down a quieter road, find a decent spot to pull over onto the shoulder and park. Before getting out, I work up the courage to send a text to the one person who can actually relate to part of what I'm feeling and then get out of the car. I carefully hike down the embankment that leads to a stretch of vacant shoreline below, my feet slipping in the sand as I descend. Once I get on level ground, I walk aimlessly along the beach until I eventually sit on the sand near the shore, taking my shoes off. I watch the waves crash one after the other by my feet, allowing the tips of my toes to get wet. I'm in a trance, processing my conversation with Brian, when I hear a "Hey," behind me. I turn to see John walking toward me, his car parked behind mine up on the hill.

"Hi," I say softly, smiling up at him, but it must not be very convincing, because his face falls as soon as he gets close enough to see my expression.

"Are you kidding me? Did he hurt you already? I knew this was a bad idea," he grumbles, not bothering to hide his frustration. I can't help but let out a small laugh at his outburst.

"No, he didn't hurt me. Sit down, though. I could use some advice." I motion to the sand next to me. He settles in, resting his arms on his bent legs before turning to me.

"You're freaking me out, Quinn. What's up? And why are you sending me texts asking me to meet you at some random deserted beach?" He studies me, concern obvious on his face. I blow out a breath, not exactly sure how to broach this subject. This isn't exactly an easy conversation to have with John, but I'm in a desperate place.

"We don't talk about Mom and Dad." My voice feels so small, and it's hard to push the statement out. John's mouth opens slightly, and his brows lift up in shock.

"Umm," he stammers, clearly not anticipating the direction of this conversation.

"I guess what I mean is…how do you? Talk about it. With Mia?" I look out at the ocean before continuing. "I'm sure you know this already, but I don't talk about them to anybody. Nobody. But the thing is, I want to. I feel like I need to. I just don't know how. It hurts too much."

He blows out a slow breath and runs his hand through his hair. "Listen, I'm certainly not an expert by any means, and I had my own issues with holding everything in for a long time—you know that. I don't know that I have any good advice about opening up. I just know that it feels better once you do. It feels freeing to let it all out."

I nod, soaking up his words. It's quiet for a few moments until he speaks again.

"The therapist I saw for my PTSD gave me some advice about speaking your hurt out loud. She suggested finding someone you can trust and then just start with one small thing at a time. One small memory that you let out into the open, and then eventually, try another small thing until it gets a little easier and you get comfortable sharing more. It seems silly, but you can always practice in a mirror by yourself first if that seems easier. And if it helps, I'm always here to talk." He smiles at me. "I have a lot of the same memories as you do, you know?"

I nod, letting his words sink in, and then I rest my head on his shoulder, suddenly feeling the weight of exhaustion.

"Thanks, John," my weary voice comes out just above a whisper. He wraps his arm around me in a protective way, and we sit like that for a long time, watching the ocean waves crash at our feet until the sun eventually starts to set.

22

————————

QUINN

"Are you sure you're good?" John asks me once we make it up the embankment to the road.

"I'm alright." I smile weakly. "Or at least, I think I can be." He wraps me in a hug, and I inhale a deep breath into his shirt, trying to get closer, as if he has some kind of secret strength that might rub off on me if I try hard enough.

"Let me know if you need anything, okay? I'll do whatever I can. We're a team, remember?" He squeezes my arms one last time and steps back with a gentle smile on his face.

"I remember," I say softly, returning his smile with a nod of my head. We walk back to our separate cars, and I slide into my driver's seat. I wave as John passes me onto the main road, and I turn the key to start my car. "American Girl" by Tom Petty fills my car, and I immediately squeeze my eyes shut at the song. I wasn't aware on the drive over here that I had been listening to Brian's favorite radio station. Instead of switching to a different station, I leave it on as I pull out onto the street, the familiar music starting to provide some small sense of comfort. I start aimlessly driving again, lost in my thoughts.

As I drive, listening to music that reminds me of him, I think about what Brian said to me and what it is that I really want. I don't know what the answer is or if I'm even capable of letting someone all the way in, but I do know that I'm tired of running. Tired of resisting. Of being alone. I wipe at the tears under my eyes, feeling slightly stronger after reflecting on my conversation with John. As I drive, the sun slowly goes all the way down, darkness falling. A quiet resolve eventually fuels me forward, and I know exactly where I want to go.

Before long, I'm parking in the driveway and walking carefully along the sandy path that I've walked on countless times over the past few weeks, being guided by the moonlight and faint light coming from inside the house. I knock on the door and take a deep breath, the empty hammock on the right catching my eye as I wait. A nervous energy encompasses me, as if it sits on the very surface of my skin, anticipation building at seeing him again.

When the door opens, my eyes lock with Brian's, and although he does look surprised, he doesn't say a word—neither of us do. I watch as his surprised expression morphs slowly into one of concern. Every line on his face deepens just by looking at me. My eyes fill with tears without warning, and I push my lips together, slowly shrugging my shoulders.

"I don't know how to let you in." Vulnerability and honesty seep out with my whisper. His face softens, and he steps closer to me, wrapping his arms around me, and that's all I need to fully breathe again. I wrap my own arms around his middle, turning my head to rest my cheek on his chest.

"I know," he whispers back and squeezes me tighter. We stay like that for a long time, the only sound coming from the waves crashing somewhere in the darkness behind me. At some point, he loosens his grip, running his hand up and down my back slowly.

"Let's take it one step at a time," he suggests softly, "one day at a time. No overthinking or analyzing what it all means…just let yourself feel it, okay?"

I blink away some fresh tears and look up until my eyes meet his, tightness still lingering in my chest.

"Okay." I give my best attempt at a smile, and he leans down to plant a soft kiss on my lips. I kiss him back, silently agreeing to do my best to take one day at a time.

"Do you want to stay? It's okay if you don't. I know it's late. I can drive you home if you want, too," he says quickly, clearly not wanting to push too far. But the thing is, I do. I really do. I don't have a lot figured out right now, but I do know that I just want to be near him.

"I want to stay," I confirm softly with a nod.

"You'll stay?" he repeats, his expression turning hopeful.

"I'd like to at least try," I say quietly. He smiles and takes my hand to slowly lead me inside.

"Are you hungry?" he asks, pausing by the kitchen. "Thirsty?"

"No…just tired," I admit. He nods in agreement, his eyes also looking heavy. He flips off light switches and grabs a laundry basket of folded clothes from the laundry room as we go down the hallway, tucking it under his free arm. Our journey to his room the last time was rushed, heated, and eager, but tonight it feels charged with emotion, deliberate and intentional.

"There's an extra pack of toothbrushes under the sink, and T-shirts are in the second drawer if you want something to sleep in," he says, pointing to the dresser in the right corner of his room.

"Thanks," I say with a smile, letting go of his hand to pull the drawer open. I find a large stack of T-shirts, each one with a different band name or logo on them. There's a black one on top of The Eagles, a gray Rolling Stones one underneath.

"There's a Golden Girls one at the bottom of the stack," Brian says nonchalantly from across the room as I thumb a John Mayer one. I let out a laugh, appreciating his attempt to lighten the mood with humor. He sets the laundry basket on the floor in his closet, grabbing a stack of towels to set on the bathroom counter.

"I'll settle for Bruce tonight." I pull out a dark-blue tee with Springsteen written in dark block letters across the front.

"Good choice," he says, crossing the room to stand directly in front of me. He reaches over to tuck a strand of my hair behind my ear while he studies me intently with his dark-brown eyes.

"I just need to ask again," he says in almost a whisper. "Are you sure this is okay? Staying the night?"

"I think so." I do my best to sound convincing because the truth is, I am far from certain that this is a good idea. My instincts and reflexes are telling me that this is a bad idea, and it goes against everything I've ever done. However, a smaller but more convincing part of my heart is telling me I need to at least try.

"Because I don't want you to stay if you're uncomfortable," he says. "We can wait to do all this. Back it up a few steps if that's what you need."

"I know. I want to be here, Brian. I promise," I say as I move past him, squeezing his forearm that's hanging by his side and kissing his cheek on the way. I head to the bathroom, where I brush my teeth and change. When I come out, Brian's already settled between the all-white bedding on his king-sized bed, pointing a remote at the TV.

He slides the covers down for me, keeping his focus on the remote, as if purposely trying to not draw any more attention to me and the significance of this moment. When I slide in between the crisp cotton sheets and pull the fluffy duvet on top of me, I snuggle as close as I can to his side, relishing the way he makes me feel warm in more ways than one, hoping desperately that if I stay focused on this feeling, maybe all the other feelings will stay small.

"I think it's time I introduce you to the girls," he says, pressing play on *The Golden Girls*.

"Yes!" I gasp and laugh at the same time. And we watch episode after episode, laughing at the crazy antics of the four elderly women, letting the laughter overshadow the emotions from earlier. Completely content with my leg draped over his, my arm splayed across his stomach, and the soft comfort of his bed around me, I eventually fall asleep in his arms.

23

BRIAN

"How'd you sleep?" I mumble into Quinn's hair. She's on her side, facing away from me, but she's close enough that her hair tickles my nose, and her feet just barely touch my legs. I fight the urge to pull her tighter against my torso. The absolute last thing I want to do is rock the boat or scare her off this time around. I need to tread carefully to make sure she's okay and comfortable being here with me—that's all I want.

"Mmm," she murmurs with a stretch, turning to face me. Burrowing herself closer, she tucks herself just below my chin, throwing an arm over my side.

"Good," she says quietly. I blow out a silent sigh of relief, built-up tension leaving my body because there's no sign of uneasiness in her voice. I slide my arm around her, resting the tips of my fingers on her spine.

"You sure?" I ask, needing to hear it again.

She lifts her head up until our eyes meet and gently nods her head.

"One step at a time, right?" she says softly. A hint of apprehension is trying to hide behind her eyes, which, honestly, I can empathize with. It's like the road before us is a brand-new one that neither of us quite knows how to navigate. Or what it will look like.

"That's right," I confirm. Overall, I would say that I'm feeling cautiously optimistic. After laying everything on the line at her apartment yesterday, I had been worried that I went too far. That I had just further forced her to shut me out. But I couldn't help it. I had to do it that way. If there was a chance I was going to lose her for good, I had to at least shoot my shot and tell her how I feel. Prove to her that she can let me be there for her—that I'd be good at that. Now that she's here, I'm absolutely willing to walk this path with her, no matter how complicated it will most likely be.

My only experience with grief is feeling the loss when my dad walked out on us, and my lack of respect for the man made it hard to feel much more than resentment. I don't think I have the tools to help her, but dammit, I'm going to try. Quinn deserves for me to try.

"What do you have planned for today?" she asks, looking up at me. The free-standing fan that sits in the corner of the room makes a low humming noise as it rotates back and forth, doing its job to aid the air conditioning unit in battling the humidity that's likely already rising outside.

"I'm taking a group out snorkeling today for a few hours, and then I have an evening fish charter booked." I mindlessly brush some hair away from her face as I talk, almost like it's an ingrained habit that I do without fully realizing that I'm doing it. "What about you?"

"No plans," she says, and I pick up on a hint of forced positivity, uneasiness lurking behind the words.

"Do you want to come with me? I'm sure both charters would love photos," I say, not wanting to leave her alone and possibly end up deep in her feelings by herself all day. She perks up at the offer and nods with a smile on her face.

"I'd love that, actually—if you don't mind, that is," she says.

"I'll never mind. You don't have to question that."

With one last squeeze, we climb out of bed, and I have to force myself to not be distracted by how good she looks in just my T-shirt that falls to mid-thigh on her legs. My mind flashes to the other night when she stayed over and picked up my T-shirt that had been thrown on the floor, sleeping with just that on.

My body's screaming at me to follow her into the bathroom, all the way into the shower, and to push her up against the wall, warming up the shower before the water even turns hot. But I hamper down the urge and wait respectfully on the edge of my mattress until she emerges in a towel, toothbrush in hand. Once we get dressed, we head to her apartment to grab her camera and then make our way to the marina.

"So, who's going snorkeling? Is it another family?" she asks from the passenger seat as we drive. She has one leg propped up, her arms loosely wrapped around it as she looks out the window. She has black running shorts on, a bright-yellow bikini top, and a white tank top tied loosely around her waist.

"No, it's a group excursion today. Six people total."

"It's a beautiful day for it," she says, admiring the blue sky above without a cloud in sight.

I grab her hand to weave my fingers through hers and rest them on the center console. It feels good doing something as mundane and ordinary as driving with her hand in mine. It feels natural. Like maybe I have reason to hope for us.

We make it to the marina and climb out of my truck, grabbing the cooler and supplies for the day. The ocean waves roll under the dock as we walk past the varying-sized fishing boats and sailboats, some out of the water in a lift, others tied up and floating along with the waves. She climbs right into my boat, and we work quietly in a comfortable silence, prepping everything while we wait for the clients to arrive.

"Oh, here come some people," Quinn says as a couple turns down our boat slip.

"Hi! Welcome to Brian's Deep-Sea Fishing and Excursions. I'm Quinn, Brian's first mate," she says cheerfully, and I can't help but laugh, wondering if I'm going to need to start paying her as an employee at some point. We make our introductions and wait for the rest of the group to arrive.

"Where are you guys from?" Quinn asks.

"Texas," the woman answers, having a seat next to her husband.

"Great state," Quinn responds immediately. "I went backcountry camping in Big Bend National Park once. It was amazing!"

"Wow, that's impressive. I don't think I could ever do that. Our friends have been trying to get us to do that for years," she laughs.

They make small talk while we wait, and I pull out the waiver and release contracts for the guests to sign. I have a hard time taking my eyes off Quinn and the way she lights up around people, chatting away effortlessly and fully engrossed in the conversation. It's mesmerizing to watch. When the rest of the group arrives, I go over safety procedures, and Quinn gets everyone's permission to photograph the excursion.

"This spot taken?" she asks, sliding into the seat next to me as everyone else is seated on the bench seats that run on the perimeter of the boat. I grin as I lower the boat fully into the water.

"Reserved for you," I reply. Her eyes hold mine, and something sparks in them as the corner of her mouth curves up. The smile lingers as she pulls her hair back in a bun. I shift the gear into reverse and take us out of the bay, waving in greeting to a fellow boat that's just coming in from a morning fish.

"Alright, everybody, hang on," I announce as I increase the speed, gliding the boat on top of the waves. Quinn grips the seat, and her whole face lights up with exhilaration. To my relief, she looks like the Quinn I know—carefree and untamed—no trace of the sadness or heartache from yesterday. We approach one of my favorite snorkeling spots, and I slow the boat to an idle to drop the anchor.

"Alright, guys, let me grab the gear for you," I say, reaching into a side compartment to pull out the mesh bags that house a mixed assortment of goggles, snorkel vests, and fins.

"Everything's been cleaned and sanitized. There are several different sizes of everything, so you should be able to find what you're looking for. I ask that you please wear the yellow vests, even if you don't want to inflate them, so I can keep a good headcount on all of you. It's early enough in the day that the wind is pretty minimal, so we've got great conditions for snorkeling. Let me know if you have any questions." I rub my hands together, trying to recall if I left anything out of my pre-snorkeling spiel.

"Oh, we've got bottles of water in the cooler over here. Help yourselves. You'll want to remember to stay hydrated in this heat. It's a hot one today." With that, the guests start rummaging through the gear while Quinn and I help with tightening straps on masks or pulling on fins.

"Try over there," I say to one couple when they're all geared up, "by those rocks. It's a great spot for yellow tang and triggerfish." They slide off the side of the boat and swim off with their heads under the water, the breathing tubes sticking out above the surface.

One by one, the guests all disembark and start exploring the reef below. I pick up the stray gear that's on the floor of the boat and then have a seat next to Quinn, resting my elbow on the side of the boat.

"You can go, too, if you want," I offer to her. "I have to stay and keep watch, but you go ahead if you want to."

She responds by sliding closer to me. "Nah, I'm good here with you."

Liking that answer, I slide my arm around her shoulders, and we get comfortable to spend the next hour gently bobbing up and down with the boat, counting the yellow vests in the water, and admiring the stunning view of the Oahu coastline.

24

QUINN

"Leilani, I've got Quinn! You get John!" My father calls to my mother as he sprints after me. I let out a squeal as my feet stumble in the sand, causing me to trip and land face first. I'm spitting out sand when he catches up to me, roaring with laughter.

"Are you alright, Q?" He grabs my elbow to help me up.

We are enjoying a nice afternoon at the beach, complete with a picnic lunch, beach ball tossing and this game of tag. I wipe my mouth with the back of my hand, seeing John chasing Mom out of the corner of my eye.

"Not funny!" I pout, which makes his smile grow wider.

"Aw, Quinny-bug, I'm sorry." He scoops me up and sets me on top of his shoulders, which he knows I love.

"Should we go for a swim?" he asks, and I giggle as he races toward the ocean.

I gasp, sitting up in bed with a start, tears already wet on my face. My heart rate accelerates, and the ache in my chest gets more painful with each passing second, an overwhelming and crushing weight that hit the very second I opened my eyes.

"Quinn?" Brian asks from behind me, and immediately, I'm reminded that I'm at his house. In his bed. Panic rushes up my spine, my muscles tense, and my throat starts to close because I don't know how to be here right now. How to share this space with my grief.

The mattress dips as he starts to sit up, and I instantly jump out of bed, fueled by anxiety and the deep pain in my chest that hasn't relented at all. I rush to his bathroom and shut the door behind me, sliding my back down the wall across from the sink until my knees are bent and my head hangs over them, struggling to inhale a full breath. I try to get a handle on the all-consuming grief by taking slow breaths in and out, but the tears can't be stopped. I hear the door click open, and I can vaguely see Brian's figure step inside, but everything is hazy, as if I'm still dreaming. Nothing's sharp or in focus.

"Hey," I hear his gentle voice say from somewhere on my right, and then I feel his hand on my arm. My head falls back against the wall, and I squeeze my eyes shut, tears spilling out in the process.

"I don't.... I can't..." The words don't come out right, so I give up trying to force anything out.

"It's okay," he says, his voice a little closer to me now, and I can feel his leg bump mine as he sits on the floor directly in front of me. Aware that he's so close, I instinctively lean forward into him, and he immediately wraps both arms around me. I don't have the strength to bring my arms up around him, so I just let him hold me. I can feel the tenderness and emotion pouring out of him with every caress of his finger, every tightening of his grip on my back, and even though I'm feeling such intense emotion, his touch feels gentle—secure and safe. Being held by him feels very close to being held by the two people I miss more than anything in this world, and I can't help but let out a strangled cry.

"It's okay," he repeats, bringing one hand to the back of my head. "I'm right here, Quinn."

The sobs are uncontrollable now as I let the pain surge through me, too exhausted to hold any of it back. It feels like a tidal wave is bursting inside of me, right at the surface, threatening to overflow.

"It's alright…you can go there, Quinn. Feel it," he whispers. "I've got you."

His words give me strength—not to force the pain away but to sink deeper into it. Like a current pulling me under water, I let go and let the grief take me where it wants to go. Wave after wave of agony washes over me, and I feel completely consumed by it. Every single ounce of my being is overpowered by the crushing weight of sadness. Fully consumed by this moment, I'm absolutely desperate for just one more touch, one more smile, one more conversation with them. One more chance to hear 'Quinny-bug' from that voice I love so much and will never hear again.

I sob against Brian's chest as the pain morphs into anger. Anger that they were ripped from me. That I have to live the rest of my life without them. The unfairness of it all is stifling. These aren't new feelings by any means, but the fact that I'm feeling them so deeply while in the presence of and being comforted by another person adds a whole other layer of awareness and intensity.

Brian's hands grip me tighter, a subtle reminder that he's still with me. I somehow find the energy to wrap my arms around him, pushing myself closer against him, needing to ground myself with something. Memory after memory starts to scan like a slideshow in my mind. The street corner that we sat at every year for the Floral Parade. The time Mom took me to the local mall to have my ears pierced. The chocolate sprinkle donuts Dad would come home with every Saturday morning after golfing. How Mom would make her traditional Saimin soup when John or I were sick.

After getting lost in the memories for what feels like a long time, I eventually start to become more aware of the physical space I'm in. The feel of the cold tile underneath my toes. The glare of the fluorescent light above the sink. The pulse beating through Brian's fingertips on my back. This awareness gradually pulls me out of the trenches, one painful memory at a time.

My sobs slow to shaky, erratic exhales while the tightness in my chest starts to slowly loosen. I squeeze my eyes shut, feeling myself come back to the present. When I feel steady enough, I ease my grip on Brian and start to pull back. He seems reluctant to let me go, barely relaxing his arms.

"Hey," he says, his voice low and gravelly. I wipe at my face with my fingers and then lift my gaze to meet his. When our eyes meet, he chooses this moment to remove his arms from my back and places his hands around each side of my face. He tilts my chin up slightly to ensure that my eyes will stay locked with his.

"I'm so proud of you," he whispers. His words cause fresh tears to spring at the corners of my eyes, and I take a deep breath in, let it out, and give him a sad smile. He's calm and steady, like the rock that he always is, but he also looks exhausted. Because being close to me means feeling my pain too. And there's a lot of it deep in there—that's just a sad reality of my life.

"I'm sorry," I say quietly, suddenly embarrassed at my display of emotion. His fingers twitch involuntarily against my cheeks, and he shakes his head intently.

"Don't you dare apologize," he says firmly. "I'm here for you, Quinn. Any way you need me to be." His thumb grazes the span of my cheek, causing me to lean into his hand. "You need me to hold your hand through the flashbacks? I'll do that. Every single time. You need me to give you space? I'll do that, too." He pushes his fingers through the hair around my ears, leaning forward to kiss my forehead at the same time. "But I prefer to be right here with you…if I get a vote, that is. You just tell me what you need." He smiles gently, and if I wasn't already a puddle on the floor, I sure would be after hearing those words.

It's a unique feeling, being vulnerable with my grief with someone other than my therapist for the first time. It feels raw and unnerving, like I'm exposed, every ugly and dark part of me on display for him to see. I'm not used to feeling this way, and it makes me apprehensive and uncomfortable. But every second that passes with Brian looking at me the way that he is, like this didn't scare him away in the slightest, makes the uneasiness gradually melt away. Eventually, the only thing I feel is exhausted, completely and utterly depleted from the depth of emotion that I just experienced.

"Here, let me help you," Brian says when I attempt to move. He stands first and pulls me gently to my feet, my legs feeling weak and wobbly. He steadies me with his hands on either side of my ribcage. When he's convinced I can stand on my own, he lets me go so he can turn the shower on.

"Can I?" he asks, gesturing to his T-shirt I'm wearing. My lips manage to lift into a small smile as I realize what he's doing. He's taking care of me. And not a single part of me wants to stop him from doing so. So, I nod. He lifts the shirt over my head, then guides me over to the shower. He doesn't attempt to get in with me or try to steal glances at my body as I step in—he just helps me in.

"I'll be right outside the door if you need me, okay? I'll grab your clothes and put them on the floor."

I can hear him shuffling around on the other side of the shower curtain, but I'm not entirely sure he can hear me over the sound of the shower when I whisper, "Thank you."

25

BRIAN

I add diced ham to the skillet, then follow up with some shredded gruyere cheese on top of that. After folding it over to make an omelet, I flip it onto the other side to cook and put the container of eggs back in the fridge while I wait. I tap my fingers impatiently on the counter and glance out the open front door for the millionth time to check on Quinn, who's sitting on the top step of the porch, holding a mug of coffee with two hands, looking out at the ocean. The thick gray blanket I brought out to her earlier is wrapped around her shoulders, her long brown hair peeking out of the top.

I'm used to taking care of those around me and doing things for others, but this is completely different. I'm not doing this out of a sense of obligation or just to be a nice guy, like I do with everyone else. I'm taking care of Quinn because I feel this deeprooted need for her to be okay. I've come to realize that her happiness and well-being are directly correlated to my own.

I inhale a deep breath, feeling somewhat sluggish from the lingering effects of this morning. The intensity of it all. When she was breaking down in the bathroom, I was breaking down at the same time, too. Not for the same reasons, of course. I couldn't feel the depth of pain she was feeling, but I was completely ruined in my own way just by watching her feel it. It absolutely gutted me. When she loosened her grip on me, I had to tamper down the urge to say not yet—she may have been ready to let me go, but I wasn't ready to let her go. I needed her reassurance just as much as she needed mine in that moment.

On the one hand, a part of me is honored that she felt comfortable enough with me to allow me to be with her through it—that she trusted me enough. But on the other hand, it's devastating that this is her reality. That this kind of pain exists within her and is something she deals with often—and all by herself.

I pour some orange juice into a small glass and take a plate from the cupboard, grabbing the pan and sliding the omelet onto it. I top it with some chopped chives and put a cluster of grapes next to it. Just as I'm reaching for the silverware drawer, my phone rings, and the name *Ethan* appears on the screen. I had called him earlier when Quinn was in the shower, but he hadn't answered at the time.

"Hey," I say quietly, bringing the phone to my ear, walking farther down the hall, so Quinn doesn't hear me through the open door.

"What's up?" he asks casually with a grogginess in his voice that tells me he just woke up.

"I need your help today," I tell him.

"I thought you didn't have anything booked today?"

"I don't. I was planning on doing some maintenance on the boat today to make sure it's in top shape for the tournament, but something came up, and I can't do it anymore. Can you head to the marina sometime today and get a few things done for me, please?" I ask. There's silence for a moment and some rustling as if he's sitting up. I don't explain that the thing that came up is Quinn, and there's no way I'm leaving her alone today.

"You want me to do it?" He sounds surprised.

"Yes. Please. Just a few basic things—change the oil, check the coolant in the motor, and check the on-board fire extinguisher system. I know I'm usually the one to handle these things, so if you need help, Zeke should be around today. I'll let him know you'll be there."

"I can handle it," he replies with a little more energy behind his voice.

"Thanks. I really appreciate it. Let me know if you have any issues, okay?"

"You got it."

I hang up, ignoring the nagging voice in the back of my mind that's questioning whether I can fully trust him or not, and grab the omelet and juice. When I reach the step where she's sitting, I set the plate and cup next to her, handing her a fork.

"This looks delicious, thank you," she says softly, setting her coffee down to grab the plate. "You didn't have to make me breakfast."

"I know. I wanted to," I reply, gazing out at where some birds are flying above the waves. Out of the corner of my eye, I can see her take a bite and then slowly turn her head to peer at me.

"You don't have to worry about me," she says guiltily. "I can see it on your face, you know. Is your jaw sore from clenching it so much?"

"I'm not clenching." I frown, suddenly becoming aware of the tension that's gripping several places in my body.

"You definitely are. You do that, you know. Clench your jaw when you're worried or stressed about something. But I'm okay. I promise," she says sincerely, sliding a grape in her mouth, then she sets the plate down next to her before turning back to me.

"It's not always that intense," she explains softly. "The memories. The grief. I just didn't know how to be around someone else and feel it all, you know? I'm usually by myself in the mornings when it hits me, so I have my own ways of coping with it. I'm not used to someone else being there, and I guess I kind of spiraled." She looks down, then back up. "So, thank you. For being there. For holding me through it." Her voice cracks a little with emotion, and her eyes bore into mine, a new layer of depth behind the warm brown hue of her irises.

As painful as this morning was, it definitely brought us to a new level. She was brave enough to face her deep-rooted pain, and we're now bonded by the simple fact that she trusted me enough to be there with her through it.

"There's nothing to thank me for," I reply earnestly, holding her eye contact. "I didn't do anything except be there. But I'll do that every single time if you need me to."

"I suppose we can say that we're officially past the casual line now." She cringes and laughs sheepishly. I don't join her in laughing or smiling back, focusing intently on the truth of that statement.

"I crossed that line a while ago, Quinn."

She gives me a half-smile and then scoots as close as she can to my side, sliding her arm around my back, allowing me to join her under the blanket. She leans into me, resting her head against my upper arm.

"You sure you don't have anything you need to do today?" she asks.

"Not a single thing," I reply.

We're quiet for a while, watching as two kayaks a little ways out make their way in the opposite direction toward the stretch of beach where the rows of bungalows and cottages end and tiki bars and beachside hotels begin.

"Want to walk with me?" I ask, turning my head slightly to

rest my chin on top of her head. The aroma of coconut and vanilla fills my senses, and I take a full breath in, reveling in it. In her.

"Sure." She rises to stand, letting the blanket fall, like she's suddenly ready for a change of scenery. I pick up the blanket and coffee mug while she grabs the plate.

"Ooh, do you mind if I grab my camera quick?" A tiny flash of excitement appears on her face—the first I've seen all day.

"Not at all."

"I'm dying to get behind the lens and just capture something…can we go to that outlook on your property again? It had an amazing view. Unless you had other ideas."

"Nope, that sounds great." I tidy up the kitchen while Quinn gets ready. Meeting her by the door, I hold out my hand. She swings her camera strap over her head, so it lays over her cream romper. Her white bikini top is visible underneath, and her brown hair is falling loose and wavy.

She entwines her fingers with mine, and we head out onto the sand. We take the same path as last time, starting on the beach by the water.

"So, are you all ready for the fishing tournament? That's on Saturday, right?" she asks as we walk, dodging seashells as we go.

"Yeah, Saturday. There are a few things that Ethan's working on today to make sure the boat is in prime condition. I already have a plan for bait and an idea of where I want to go, so there's not a ton left to do, really."

"I'm so excited for you. I bet you'll do great. I'll pray to the fish gods that you catch a massive one." She smiles and squeezes my hand.

"I appreciate that," I chuckle.

As we walk, I'm reminded that the last time we were in this exact spot, she mentioned not planning on staying in Hawaii. I know that's a conversation we'll eventually need to have, but I hold off for now. That can be addressed another time. We've had enough heaviness for the day. I lead her up through the grassy path until we're on the hill that overlooks the small bay. Quinn releases my hand, reaching for her camera.

"Ahhh, I love it up here." She spins around, a huge grin on her face, with her signature carefree look that I admire so much. Then, she raises the camera and takes a few shots of the surrounding landscape.

"You wanna dive in?" I ask halfheartedly, gesturing toward the drop-off cliff on the edge that drops directly into the ocean. I know that she thrives on spontaneity and thrill, so I hardly think and can't help myself from saying it out loud.

Her face lights up, and she squeals. "Oh my gosh, that's such a good idea!"

"I was kidding," I laugh nervously, suddenly regretting my attempt to make her happy.

"Oh no, you can't take it back now." She grins at me, a challenge in her eye that completely erases any other emotion that was there before. She swings the camera over her head, setting it down gently, and then shimmies her romper off, momentarily distracting me from what I just inadvertently volunteered for.

"Quinn," I say, coming back to my senses, "I don't even know if this is a safe place to dive."

"I'll check it out." She shrugs, making her way toward the ledge.

"You absolutely will not," I say firmly, an overprotective urge taking over. I walk to where she's standing and peer down at the waves crashing wildly against the base of the cliff. They slam into the lava rock, spraying gusts up into the air as the wave recedes back out, making way for the next wave that's right on its heels.

"Don't move," I say pointedly to her, attempting to convey my seriousness.

"Are you jumping first?" she asks, confused.

"Hell no." I walk back to the side of the cliff where there's a natural decline and a somewhat easy path down.

"I'm checking it out," I call over my shoulder.

I make my way down the jagged rock, stopping when my feet step into the water. When I peer up at where Quinn is standing, she gives me a small wave. I can see her smile from here, and I shake my head, wondering how I got myself into this situation, but still, I can't help the smile that pulls at my lips in return.

The tide is high today, so there's a good amount of water covering the rocks below the surface. After assessing the water as best I can, I head back up.

"Okay," I say to her when I reach the top. "If you jump from right here"—I lead her to the edge, a bit to the right of where she was—"and jump that way, you'll be good. There aren't any rocks in that spot."

She follows where I'm pointing and grins over at me.

"You want to jump together?"

"I can think of about a hundred things I would rather do than jump off this cliff," I reply flatly, which only makes her grin bigger.

"Oh, it'll be exhilarating, though." The dare in her eye is holding me captive, and I can't look away. I let out a small sigh because this girl has been pushing me out of my comfort zone since we started this whole thing, and I already know I'll give in just like I have all the other times. I never really stood a chance.

"Alright, let's do it." My smile grows to match hers, and I pull my T-shirt over my head, leaving me in just my black swim trunks. I grab her hand and step forward until our toes are dangling over the ledge, and my heart starts beating faster, adrenaline rushing through me. Quinn leans up and plants a kiss on my cheek.

"Ready?" she asks a little breathily.

I can only nod in response, adrenaline getting caught in my throat.

"One…two…three."

26

____

QUINN

On the count of three, my feet push off first. Brian's follow a half second later. I squeeze his hand as we free-fall faster and faster, a thrilling rush surging through me as we fall through the air. I brace myself, plug my nose, and squeeze my eyes shut seconds before we hit the water, plummeting well below the surface. I swirl around for a moment, getting swept up in the force of the water before realizing that I'm not holding Brian's hand anymore, having been separated when we went under. I swim to the surface, looking around to see Brian emerging shortly after.

"Are you okay? Did you hurt anything?" he asks immediately, grabbing my face, then running his hands down my arms, inspecting me for injuries. I laugh and smooth the hair out of my face, sliding it behind my ears.

"I'm good. That was amazing!" I say, breathing heavily, adrenaline still rushing through me. I didn't know how much I needed that surge of excitement. Needed something exhilarating to contrast the dark feelings from this morning. I lean on spontaneous, haphazard things like this to help ground me back to reality, to feel something other than sadness.

We grin at each other, waves crashing against our bodies, before turning to swim to shore. Brian reaches the rocky path first and reaches a hand back to help me walk on them and out of the water. He doesn't let go as he leads me up the path until we get back up to the top of the cliff.

"See, that wasn't so bad, was it?" I tease him, playfully shoving his arm. His arm crosses his body, shielding himself from me with a laugh. He flexes his muscles, which causes his ink to stretch. The sound he makes when he clears his throat brings my attention away from his arm.

"I kinda want to go again," he says quietly, with a hesitant look on his face, like he's not fully understanding why he's feeling this way.

"That's the spirit," I laugh, clapping my hands together. "Let's do it!"

"What have you turned me into?" Brian asks, shaking his head but walking to the edge of the cliff entirely of his own accord. I follow behind him, thoroughly pleased that he's enjoying this.

"Hey, don't blame me. I didn't push you over the edge."

"Uh, you kinda did," he chuckles, then lowers his voice. "You should know by now that it's hard for me to say no to you." His words send a rush of warmth through my chest as I catch up to him.

"I did not know that…but that's very good information to know going forward." I wrap my hand around his forearm as it hangs by his side. He turns and leans in, giving me a gentle kiss just as a strong breeze rushes into us, and I grip his arm tighter to steady myself, still connected to him by our kiss. When he breaks away, he lifts his arm to grab my hand.

"You coming with me?" he asks, inching forward to the very edge.

"Absolutely," I respond, lining myself up next to him, and this time, Brian counts to three before we jump.

"Eeeh!" I squeal, my legs inadvertently kicking back and forth as I free-fall through the air. Brian is to my right but farther below me, gravity pulling him slightly faster than me. The wall of the ocean comes up quickly, and I barely have time to plug my nose before plunging into it.

"Ah, that never gets old," I gasp when I surface and locate Brian treading water behind me. I bob under the water and come up with my head at an angle, letting the water force my hair back along the back of my neck. When I open my eyes, I find Brian watching me, his dark-brown eyes so consuming I can't look away. They pierce into mine with layered intensity, the way they always do, but when a sly smirk creeps across his face, it causes a shiver to run down my spine.

He swims closer to where I am, lurking with his chin and part of his mouth under the water as if I'm his prey. When he reaches me, I feel his two hands grip the backs of my thighs and lift me to wrap them around him.

"What are you doing?" I ask playfully, wrapping my arms around his broad shoulders. His hands slide up my thighs, coming to a stop just under my butt, and I can feel his muscles flexing from supporting my weight. He shrugs nonchalantly.

"Thought you might be tired. Maybe need a lift back?"

"Is that right?" The tips of my fingers brush against the solid skin of his upper back.

"Just being a gentleman." He starts moving us toward the rocks, but at a snail's pace.

"Are we going to make it out of here sometime today?" I tease, running my hand up the back of his neck.

"Just taking my time. You're pretty comfortable." He squeezes the backs of my legs.

"Mmhmm," I hum in sarcastic agreement as I lower my head to hover my lips right in front of his.

"So are you," I murmur, then close the gap to press my mouth to his. He shifts, so one of his arms slides all the way under me, hoisting me farther up, while the other hand runs up the center of my back, tucking his fingers under the strap of my bikini top. He struggles to keep us afloat, and water splashes against our faces as we dip before breaking apart.

"Come on," I laugh, separating myself from him. "I don't want to drown you today."

"Woulda been worth it," he growls, spitting some water out of his mouth and swimming after me toward the rocks. We climb out and walk back up the side of the cliff, water dripping off of us with each step.

"Oh, I have a great idea," I say as soon as we reach the top. I walk to where I dropped my belongings and use my romper to dry myself off, knowing that it'll dry quickly in this heat. I grab my camera and turn around with a grin.

His face falls.

"Oh, no. I thought I said no to posing for you."

"You did, but I think you should make an exception. I really want to go over there and shoot you diving," I say excitedly. "Please?"

He roams my face, and I watch as he sighs, visibly giving in.

"What do you want me to do?" he asks.

"Just jump or dive like you normally would!" I kiss him on the cheek before skipping away. "I'll let you know when I'm ready, okay?"

I practically jog over to the far side of the cliff, just past the rocky path that we climbed up, and onto another cliff that's not quite as high as the other one. Crouching down, I bring the camera to my eye, taking a couple practice shots to check position and lighting. After adjusting the shutter speed, I look back up.

"Perfect!" I call to Brian, who's already moved closer to the edge. "Go ahead when you're ready!"

He proceeds to back up and get a running start before diving head-first over the edge. I smile as I snap pictures, appreciating the extra effort he put into the dive. When he emerges from the ocean, I can't help but snap obsessively when he walks up the rocky path. I get one of him looking down, one hand at the back of his head, the dark tattoos that span the entire length of both arms on full display without his shirt on. Another shot of him noticing me and rolling his eyes, and then a series of him grinning and in various stages of shaking his head, all with the dark lava rock and turquoise ocean rolling behind him.

Despite wanting to call out words of encouragement, I don't push my luck by saying anything as he passes in front of me. I just watch as he reaches the top and walks toward the ledge again. I spend the next half hour snapping image after image of him jumping or diving in various forms.

"Okay, you can stop." I smile and meet him the next time he walks up the path. "That was so cool. I got several of you in mid-air on the way down. Those are gonna be amazing."

"Happy to help," he says, although I pick up on some slight sarcasm. I set my camera back in its case and then wrap my arms around his waist as we slowly walk to the middle of the cliff, not in a hurry as we soak in the view and the sunshine. We come to a stop, and he gently removes my arms in order to slide me in front of him. He brings both arms over my chest, resting his chin on top of my head. I smile, shimmying back into his chest, and bring my hands up to tuck them between his arms.

Words don't feel necessary as we stand like that, looking out at the ocean in front of us, taking in the beauty of it all. I take a deep breath and think about how this morning seems so long ago, and doing this with Brian was exactly what I needed today.

27

QUINN

"Here's your cold brew with sweet cream foam. Enjoy!" I hand the drink to the woman on the other side of the counter, who's in cut-off jean shorts and a purple bikini top. The coffee shop has been packed this morning with a steady stream of customers needing their morning caffeine fix or one of Julie's famous homemade muffins. There's finally enough of a lull that I can steal a sip from my own drink—an iced coffee with a splash of cream and sugar. The lull doesn't last more than a solid minute before the entrance door swings open again.

"Aloha," Julie says warmly to the woman and little blonde girl that just walked in. "What can I get you?"

"I'll have a tall caramel macchiato, and she'll have a hot chocolate, please," the woman says kindly. I get started on the macchiato while Julie takes her payment, and my mind automatically wanders to when I was little, and my mom would take me shopping. We'd always stop at a coffee shop on the way, and she'd get me a hot chocolate with whipped cream and extra sprinkles on top. I think it was intentional on her part because, from what my aunt tells me, I was a very strong-willed child, and shopping for clothes with me was much easier if I had a treat in my hands to distract me.

My chest tightens at the memory but hovers just below the line of overwhelming. I've been noticing that memories have been popping up more frequently the past couple days. I know without a doubt that it's because being on that bathroom floor with Brian changed me. It cracked my heart wide open. I let him into my heart that day—the good, the bad, the ugly. I didn't hold anything back, just let it all pour out of me.

Now that my grief knows what it's like to not be so tightly locked down, the memories have been floating to the surface much more frequently than they used to—and it hasn't been nearly as jarring when they do. Memories that used to stop me in my tracks are now a little easier to walk through. I know that I owe that to Brian. I'll never be able to thank him enough for giving me a safe space to feel it all. To let it all out. I didn't fully know how much I needed to. How much of a freeing effect it would have on me.

"Here you go." I hand the drink to the mom and whip up the hot chocolate for the girl. I wink at her when I set it on the counter within her reach, then wave as they walk away.

"Oh, Quinn"—Julie turns to me when the door closes behind them—"I'm working on next month's schedule, so I need to know your general availability sometime within the next couple days, please."

"Okay, sure, I can do that," I reply. I typically let Julie know my tentative travel schedule at the beginning of the month, and luckily for me, she's been pretty flexible with moving me around when needed if my travel plans change, which they often do. "I'll take a peek at my calendar tonight and let you know!"

"Perfect, thank you…you're off at eleven, right?" she asks, twisting her wrist to check her Apple watch.

"Yes."

"Why don't you take off a little early? It's quieted down enough, and Brenna will be here any minute for her shift. Go enjoy the sunshine!" she says with a smile.

"Okay, great! Thanks, Julie." I grab my drink and slide my apron off as I walk around the corner to the breakroom. After grabbing my purse and saying a quick goodbye to Julie, I step out into the thick, humid air, slide my sunglasses on to shield the sun, and pull out my phone to send a message.

Quinn: Got done early!

Tori: Perfect—on my way, meet you there! Order me a marg?

Quinn: Blended? On the rocks? Spicy? Strawberry?

Tori: Surprise me!

I walk along the crowded sidewalk, skirting around a couple with hands full of souvenir bags from the local gift shop up the street and a teenager with an ice cream cone melting down his hand. After crossing the road, I pull open the door of The Toasted Crab, relishing the gust of cool air that hits my face. The crowded bar is bustling with activity, the majority of the tables and stools filled with people. Ultimately deciding on some fresh air, I walk through the bar and out the doors on the left that lead to an outdoor patio area that overlooks the beach, complete with an awning and outdoor fans.

"What can I get you?" the waitress asks, placing a cocktail napkin in front of me as I slide into the chair and set my purse on top of the table.

"Two spicy margaritas, please. Thank you so much." I watch

the many beach-goers in front of me while I wait—some trudging through the sand, others lounging on beach towels or building sand castles. There's a kid flying a green alligator kite, holding the string up as he runs in between people. I think of Julie's question earlier about my schedule, and my mind wanders to the trip I've been debating taking soon but haven't yet pulled the trigger to book.

"Hi!" Tori calls from behind me as she leans over to give me a quick hug and then settles into the seat across from me with a sigh.

"What are you thinking about? Looks serious," she says with a curious frown.

"Oh, nothing, really…just thinking about my next trip. Part of me has been dying to just bite the bullet and book this eight-day wildlife safari in Tanzania that I've had my eye on for a few years now. I found a couple great deals on a travel website, and I've got some airline miles that are set to expire soon, so I should really use them up while I can."

She eyes me suspiciously. "But something's holding you back?"

I shrug my shoulders, but before I can open my mouth to respond, she pipes in.

"Would your budding romance with Brian have anything to do with your hesitation?" she asks with a knowing smile.

I roll my eyes but smile at the same time, not bothering to hide the ounce of truth in what she said.

"I don't know…I mean, this is honestly the first trip where I'll actually have something—or someone, for that matter—that I'll miss while I'm there. It'll be hard being away from him, you know?"

"Girl, you're falling hard. You're considering staying home for a guy? I've never seen this side of you."

"That makes two of us," I laugh. "I don't know. I'll probably still go. I don't want to be the kind of girl who changes her entire life for a guy. I don't want to miss out on opportunities and things I love doing just because I don't want to be away from him. I'm just saying I'll miss him, that's all." I can feel a hint of a blush creep across my cheeks as Tori shakes her head in amusement with a goofy smile on her face.

"Never thought I'd see the day," she muses. "But honestly, I think you should go if you want to. As long as I've known you, you've always been on the move and off jet-setting somewhere new. You love it, right?"

"I really do," I admit, thinking of how much my soul comes alive when I'm traveling. How I get a specific rush from exploring somewhere new that I don't get from doing anything else.

"And I doubt Brian would want you to change who you are just for him. He seems too sensible for that."

"I know he would want me to go," I agree. "He's the epitome of supportive."

"I can totally see that," she says as the waitress returns to set our margaritas on the table.

"Thank you," we both say, then clink them together in a cheers before taking the first sip.

"Anyway, enough about me. How are things with you?" I ask.

"Pretty good. Work has been crazy. The real estate market is so hot right now. I feel like all I do is run from one showing to another, and if I'm not doing that, I'm at my desk, writing up contracts and offers. It's never-ending."

"That's a good problem, right? Keeps life interesting," I respond, taking another sip.

"That's true. I wouldn't mind if life were a little less interesting sometimes, though," she laughs. "I do have the evening off tonight. The whole fam is heading over to Ava's house for dinner."

"That'll be fun. I love your family." Besides her brother,

Matt, Tori has three sisters, Ava being one of them. And, man, are they a hoot when they're all together. It's like being inside a big feminine whirlwind that's full of sarcasm and boundary-crossing actions—most of which are directed at Matt. It's a beautiful thing to witness.

"Wanna go get açaí bowls after this? Something healthy to balance out the margaritas?" she asks with a laugh.

"Let's do it."

28

———————

BRIAN

"I booked a trip to Africa today."

The words fly quickly out of Quinn's mouth from the passenger seat of my truck. My head swivels to her at the abruptness of her statement. She's staring at me nervously out of the corner of her eye, biting at the corner of her lip.

"You what?" I huff out a laugh, grabbing her hand to try and calm her obvious jitters. I place our hands on top of her thigh, using my left hand to steer.

"I've been going back and forth on booking my next trip, but I decided to just bite the bullet and book it. I leave next week for about ten days." She cringes.

My stomach drops at the thought of not seeing her for that long, but the thing that I focus on is how she seems so unsure about it.

"And why aren't you happy about it?" I ask.

"I am happy… There's just a part of me that wants to stay.

Really bad. Plus, I didn't know how you'd feel about me going," she says quietly.

"Of course I want you to go, Quinn. You love traveling," I tell her firmly, making eye contact before continuing. "I want you to chase your dreams. All of them. Even if I'm not with you when you do."

She smiles sadly. "But I'll miss you."

My heart squeezes in my chest, and my mouth curves up into a smile. Then, I breathe in a steadying breath to work up the courage to bring up the topic I've been dancing around lately.

"I'll miss you, too. But honestly, I think the bigger question is what you're planning to do after this trip? Long-term. I know you were talking about moving on. Have you thought about where you'll go?" A small rush of nerves grip my stomach, anxious for what her response might be. I'll support her no matter what—that's a given—but I can't help but hope that she'll stay a little longer before moving away. Or hell, maybe it's not too out of reach to hope that she'd stay altogether. Her sigh is forceful before she lets out a groan.

"I don't know. There are a lot of things up in the air, to be honest. Where do I want to live? How does this whole photography thing fit in?" She pauses, then says in a lower voice, "You. Ugh. I'm kind of a mess, aren't I?"

"You're not a mess," I chuckle. "You just have some soul-searching to do." I squeeze her hand, wanting to offer assurance. "Just know that I'll be here while you take the time to do it."

"Why are you so sweet?" She rests her head against the back of the seat, tilted at an angle to look at me. "How come I never knew how sweet you were? John never mentioned your sweet side."

"John was never exactly the target of my affectionate side," I reply dryly, to which she laughs.

"Speaking of John... This'll be the first time we're all

together with everybody knowing about us. Are you nervous?" she asks.

"Not even a little bit. The only person whose opinion matters to me now is yours."

She seems to like that answer. I catch the hint of a smile before I pull into the entrance of Kualoa Ranch, a four-thousand-acre private nature reserve where we plan to spend the afternoon exploring in an open-air UTV Raptor—a "utility task vehicle," similar to an ATV, that can hold several passengers. It's ideal for trekking around and exploring the reserve.

"Are you nervous?" I ask the same question, glancing at her before pulling into a parking space.

"Nope," she says, leaning to give me a kiss on the cheek. Her voice exudes confidence, but something in her eyes flickers with the tiniest bit of unease. My foot is just stepping onto the pavement when Matt's Jeep pulls in next to us.

"Hi!" Paige says as she steps out. John and Mia pull into a spot on the other side of the lot just a second later. Quinn comes around my truck, where the six of us convene in a semi-circle in the space between our vehicles.

"Who's ready to get muddy?" Matt claps his hands together, sliding them back and forth like sandpaper. It's hard not to notice Mia's stare as she swings her eyes back and forth between Quinn and me, silently analyzing every slight movement between us. I slide my arm around Quinn's waist, my fingers rubbing against the slippery fabric of her workout tank. I do this partly to give Mia something to obsess over but also to ease any lingering doubt in Quinn's mind. An admittedly bold move without hesitation that hopefully conveys my level of comfort with her. With us.

I stifle a laugh at the widening of Mia's eyes and recognize the moment when John's gaze catches on my hand, and he does a slight double-take. To his credit, he moves on quickly, though, which I appreciate.

"Who else wants to drive the UTV?" Quinn asks as we start walking. "Because I definitely do!"

"Ladies first," Matt replies, "but I call second. We got a babysitter for this—I want to make it worth it."

"Third," John and I say at the same time, which results in him playfully jabbing my ribs with his elbow. I retaliate with a headlock, and pretty soon, we're mauling each other, nearly falling over as we eventually make it to the main building.

"Alright, that's enough," Mia says, rolling her eyes at us before changing the subject. "Thanks again for coming with me, guys. This'll be fun!"

She's writing a feature article on the Kualoa Ranch for her column in the newspaper and asked us all if we wanted to tag along. It's a pretty touristy thing to do, but the UTV riding is pretty cool. Plus, it does have some of the best views Oahu has to offer, in my opinion, so I was happy to tag along.

We sign our waivers and grab our helmets before the guide walks us to the small viewing room to watch the safety video. Then, he takes us to our ride for the next two hours. Quinn climbs behind the wheel, and I slide in the other side and scoot all the way next to her. Matt sits to my right, and John, Mia, and Paige all settle in the bench seat behind us.

"Everyone keep your arms and legs inside the vehicle," I say. "We don't want any injuries. I need you boys on your a-game tomorrow for the tournament."

"Sure thing, boss." Matt salutes me.

"You ready?" I ask Quinn, placing my hand on her thigh, feeling John's eyes burning into the back of my skull immediately. But the thing is, I just can't bring myself to taper down any affection toward her, even in the presence of her brother. It helps that he's my best friend, and I know him well enough to know that as long as his sister is happy, he is happy.

"Born ready!" She grins at me before pulling her neck bandana up around her nose to protect herself from the dust. I do the same and slide my sunglasses on. Our guide starts in his own vehicle, and Quinn follows behind him. There are a couple of other UTVs that trail behind us, each one with a decent amount of space between the next.

We head down the trail, the Koolau Mountains towering in the background. I grip the bar in front of me to brace myself against the bumps and turns. The guide leads us along a narrow path as we travel through one of the three valleys on the ranch, taking in the greenery and tropical vegetation as we go. We continue on and up the windy, dusty trail, venturing through the dense rainforest full of thick vegetation. Quinn takes us full throttle through a small stream, which has us all yelping and gripping harder. The thick trees start to clear as we head up a path that takes us to the top of an overlook. We stop this time, pulling next to the guide and hopping out.

"It's stunning," Paige breathes, looking out at the turquoise ocean with the massive mountains on the right, the entire view saturated with tall green palm trees and bushes.

"Here, let me take your picture," Quinn says excitedly, grabbing her camera case from the UTV.

"Stand right here," she directs the five of us into a line before rushing backward to get a good angle. "Okay, got it," she says after previewing the image and looking pleased.

"Wait, don't move," I tell the group. "Quinn, come here." I pull out my phone and hold it up high as she comes next to me.

"We need one with you in it…let's take a selfie." It's almost impossible to squeeze all six of us together in the tiny frame on my phone, and only half of John's face gets in the shot, but I manage to get a somewhat decent group picture. Then, Quinn wraps her arms around my waist in a side hug as everyone disperses to check out more of the view.

"I remember coming here as a kid," John says, and I feel Quinn's grip tighten slightly around me.

"Dad thought it was the coolest thing that they filmed

Jurassic Park here. He loved taking us on the movie tour." He glances at Quinn out of the corner of his eye with a gentle look.

Appreciation swirls in me, understanding exactly what he's doing. Quinn told me about her conversation with John on the beach. This is him testing the waters for her, bringing up their parents in a group setting without any direct pressure on her to contribute.

"Right on," Matt comments respectfully with a slight dip of his head.

"There's probably a whole box of photos somewhere with him posing inside every dinosaur's mouth," John laughs.

"He loved that," Quinn agrees quietly from under my right arm. It's small and quiet, but it's also monumental. Pride rushes through me as I squeeze her shoulder, silently acknowledging her bravery for speaking it out loud. John smiles and nods his head, maintaining eye contact with Quinn, before lifting his gaze to meet mine. We exchange a heartfelt stare, loaded with gratitude and understanding on both ends before Mia pulls his attention away.

The guide calls us back to the UTVs, and Matt jumps in the driver's seat this time. I let Quinn slide in the middle next to him and then take the seat next to her. We head back on the trail and finish out the rest of the tour, exploring all three valleys, passing roaming cattle and a group of people on a horseback tour along the way. When the vehicle is parked back by the entrance, we take off our helmets and masks.

"That was so cool. Definitely worth doing," Paige comments as we start the walk back to the parking lot.

"I agree," says Mia. "I can't wait to start writing my article."

"Alright, boys, I need you at the docks at 5:30, bright-eyed and bushy-tailed, okay?" I say. "I'll have plenty of water and snacks on board, but make sure you don't forget your sunglasses and sunscreen. You know the drill."

"You got it," Matt says, slapping me on the back before we disperse to our separate vehicles.

"Can't wait," John calls from the other side of the parking lot.

I open the passenger side door for Quinn and wait as she says her goodbyes to Mia and Paige. Then, she skips past me with a grin, climbing into the seat. I shut the door and walk around the back of my truck.

"Where to—your place or mine?" I ask as I buckle my seatbelt. We've been splitting our free time evenly between my house and her apartment the past few days, spending every possible minute we can together.

"Yours," she says decidedly, looking over at me with a smile. "That hammock is calling my name."

29

BRIAN

Beeeep.
Beeeep.
Beeeep.

The loud noise is followed by a flashing of the lights on the dash of the boat before they turn off completely, and the engine simultaneously goes dead.

"No, no, no, no, no." I jiggle the keys in the ignition, attempting to re-start the engine, but it's not bringing it back to life.

"Aghh!" I yell, slamming my hand against the steering wheel, panic rushing through me.

"What happened?" Matt calls from behind me.

"We lost power. I've got no hydraulics. No power steering. Nothing." I lift my baseball hat up and run my fingers through my hair in frustration.

"Well, that's not good," John says with his hand on one of the rods. "If we've lost power, that means we don't have anything to cool—"

"The hold where all of our fish are cooling…yes," I interrupt him sharply, shaking my head. I don't lose my temper often, but this day has been nothing short of a complete rollercoaster.

First, I got a phone call from Eric right as I was heading out the door, letting me know he couldn't make it anymore, as he had a sudden nasty case of the stomach flu. That left me scrambling to find a replacement teammate at the very last minute. Luckily, Ethan finally answered the sixth time I called him and agreed to come along. That put us behind schedule as I had to change the team information on my registration form at the marina before getting to the boat. We rushed in a frantic panic to get the hold filled with ice and the rest of the boat prepped, but thankfully, we somehow managed to be ready and line up with the rest of the boats at seven when they flagged us off.

Our luck seemed to turn around once we finally got to my top-choice coordinates, which no one had taken yet, and started putting lines in the water. So far, we've caught a couple of decent-sized ahi, and we were especially ecstatic to pull in what I'm guessing is around a five-hundred-pound marlin, which I'm hoping just might qualify for the largest marlin of the day.

This is a 'most points' tournament, which means that you earn one point for every pound of fish you catch, and then there are additional categories where you can earn extra points, like biggest marlin or biggest ahi of the day. At the weigh-in this evening, the money will be distributed to the three highest-scoring teams. But none of that matters if we don't have power to keep the hold where we keep the fish cool.

"So, you're telling me we're ninety miles from shore and dead in the water?" Matt asks.

"Yup. Pull the lines up," I say, squeezing past Ethan to access the tiny mechanical room below, where the on-board generator system functions. I try to get a read on the situation, but at first glance, nothing looks out of place to me. All of the fuses in the panel look fine, and so do the wire connections at the back. Everything seems to be connected and working as it should.

"I'm not seeing anything obvious," I say. "There's a flashlight in the glovebox. Can somebody grab it for me?"

After John hands it to me, I shine the light to get a better look at the back of the unit, but again, everything appears normal.

"Let me look," Ethan says over my shoulder.

"Ethan, please," I dismiss him, the stress of the day catching up to me.

"I'm serious…let me look."

"Alright," I give in, officially at a loss for what the problem is. I move out of the way to let him pass, grabbing the back of the captain's chair to steady myself as the boat bobs with the waves. I try turning the keys in the ignition again to no avail.

"Should we call the Coast Guard?" John asks.

"Just give me a minute before you do that. I think I know what the problem is," Ethan says.

"You do?" I ask in surprise.

"Maybe…" His voice trails off, fully focused on the generator. John, Matt, and I exchange glances when he shifts the generator forward to peer behind it.

"Yup," Ethan says, "found it."

"What do you mean you found it? Found what?" I ask, coming behind him to look over his shoulder.

"One of the main power wires is frayed, causing a short in the system."

My confusion is two-fold. Confusion over how I would have missed that, and then confusion over who this confident person in front of me is because he sounds nothing like my little brother.

"Alright, let me fix it," I say.

"I can do it," he assures me, reaching for some electrical tape, splicers, and some plastic parts from the small toolbox I have on board. I decide to listen to the voice in my head that's telling me to trust him, even though another voice is reminding me that this boat is very expensive and what my entire business and livelihood is centered around. I crouch next to him, observing as he works on the wire. After about fifteen minutes, he closes the toolbox and shifts the generator back into place, closing the hatch.

"Alright, press the master power button and turn the key on —see if it works," he says. I twist the key, and sure enough, the engine rumbles to life.

"Nice, man," Matt says, giving the back of Ethan's shoulder a good pat.

"How did you know it was a wire?" I ask him.

"Just a hunch." He shrugs. "My buddy, Aaron, and I have been refurbishing old boats in our spare time, so I guess stuff like this is just fresh in my mind."

"Since when?" I ask, opening the hold to ensure that it's cooling properly.

"The last couple weeks. It's been fun," he says nonchalantly.

"Well, I'd say we owe you one," John says. "Think the wire will hold the whole way back?"

"It should," Ethan says under his breath with another shrug.

"We'll find out. We gotta start heading back if we want to make it back by four," I say, glancing at my watch.

"Let's go," Matt responds. I shift the boat into gear, and we start cruising back inland, one choppy wave at a time. Now that the crisis has been averted and we're on our way back in, excitement starts buzzing through me at the thought of weighing our catches at the marina. We might actually have a shot at placing in the top three.

Eventually, we reach the marina, and I slow to an idle and get in line behind another boat near the weigh dock. We watch as an ahi is being off-loaded with the crane two boats ahead of us. One by one, the boats move forward, each one taking their turn unloading their catches. We watch and speculate on the size of the fish. Finally, I ease up next to the weigh dock while the guys get the ropes ready to tie up to the dock.

"Any final guesses?" Matt asks as the crane lifts our marlin up into the air.

"Four hundred fifty pounds," John guesses.

"Five hundred," I guess. The numbers rapidly increase on the large display monitor on the right side of the building.

Three hundred.

Four hundred.

Four seventy-five.

Five hundred ten pounds reads the final number.

"Yeah!" Matt and John cheer from behind me, and a grin grows wide on my face. It's not the biggest marlin I've ever caught, but definitely the biggest one I've caught in a tournament.

The ahi gets off-loaded as well, and then we circle around to pull into my dock slip. We tie the boat up, figuring we'll come back after the ceremony to wash the boat and put it on the lift. We spend a few minutes cleaning and stowing gear on the boat and then step onto the dock to head over to the small reception that's set up near the parking lot, where they'll announce the results.

I see Quinn before I hear her. She's a blur of black as she's practically sprinting toward us, dodging other people on the dock.

"Eeek!" She jumps straight onto me, wrapping her arms and legs around me in one fluid movement. I clutch her thigh, holding her up from underneath with one hand, smiling into her hair that's blowing across my face.

"Congratulations!" she squeals, peppering kisses all over my face.

"We don't know the results yet," I chuckle, not putting much effort into resisting her. She pulls back to connect her eyes with mine.

"It doesn't matter. This is exciting no matter what," she says breathlessly. "Doesn't it just give you a thrill?" She makes no effort to move, so I walk with her still clinging to me until we make it to the reception area where Mia, Paige, and the kids are.

"I'm gonna take off," Ethan says.

"You're not gonna stick around?" I turn to him after Quinn climbs off of me.

"Nah." He shrugs. "See ya later."

I can barely mutter a thank you before he's already halfway to his car and out of earshot. Eventually, the last of the boats make their way back, and the tournament leader steps up onto the small podium.

"First, I want to say thank you to all of the participants in the tournament today. We appreciate your sportsmanship and your support of the sport-fishing industry," he says. "Now, I won't keep you too long. Let's get right to the point of what you're all waiting for. I'll run through and announce the points for ahi and then for marlin."

He starts with ahi and goes down the list, announcing the points for each boat. We listen with bated breath to each number he calls. Based on the points for the ahi, our team is tied for first place with a fellow boat. The tie-breaker will come down to the size of the marlin we both caught. Shock consumes me when he announces the size of the other team's marlin—four hundred seventy-three pounds. Which means our five hundred ten pounder solidifies our spot in first place. The first place slot that will win ninety thousand dollars.

30

QUINN

"Have you thought about what you'll do? With the money?" I ask from under Brian's left arm, where I'm tucked close, both of my arms wrapped around his torso. He uses his right hand to grip the tongs, turning the pieces of steak that are marinating in the bowl on his kitchen island.

"Not yet," he replies. "I think I'm going to sit on it for a while before making any big decisions."

"Does that mean you're rethinking getting another boat?" I release him to grab the kabob skewers off the counter.

"Maybe. Maybe not. I just want to make sure I've put some thought into it and do what's best for me and the business as a whole, and not just make an impulsive decision that's driven mostly by an attempt to help Ethan out, ya know?"

I smile, feeling both impressed and proud that he's putting himself first.

"I think that sounds like a solid plan." I start assembling the kabob pieces onto the skewers one at a time. First, a chunk of bell pepper, followed by a pineapple slice, steak piece, and then an onion wedge. I repeat that order until the skewer is full, then place it on a large plate that Brian just pulled out from a cabinet in the island.

"What would you do with the money if you won it?" he asks, coming to help me assemble the kabobs.

"Hmm," I ponder, "probably travel the world. Hit every single place on my bucket list."

"Why does that not surprise me?" he chuckles.

"That reminds me, how's your travel jar coming along?" I peer behind his back to glance at the jar still sitting in the same place on the counter that now has several bills crumpled inside. "I see you've been adding to it." The rush of happiness the sight of the jar gives me is something I can't put into words.

"Slowly but surely. Maybe I'll use some of the money to travel with you someday," he suggests with a wiggle of his eyebrows.

"Don't tease me like that." I give him a warning look, to which he laughs.

"Do you want to come with me to Africa?" I say excitedly, grabbing the empty bowls and placing them in the sink behind me. "There's still time to book."

"I wish I could, but I can't be gone from the business for that long. Besides, I'd need to plan it out a little further in advance to block out my charter schedule and stuff like that." He smiles and leans over to kiss me gently on the lips.

"But let's plan something else. I'd love to go on vacation with you."

"Deal." I grin. "I'll even let you pick where we go."

"Perfect. Do you mind getting the door?" he asks. I skirt past him to beat him to the front door and open it for him as he walks past me with the plate. He turns right to get to the grill that's situated on the far side of the porch. I have a seat on the porch swing that's on the front wall of his house, perfectly angled out toward the ocean, while he turns the propane on.

"Beautiful evening, isn't it?" he asks, having a seat next to me, waiting for the grill to heat up as I slowly use the top of my toe to swing us back and forth. I nod in agreement, admiring the peaceful roll of the ocean waves as they settle gently on shore, the very beginning of the sunset starting to descend above the horizon line.

"I made a decision," I tell him, bringing up the first thing that pops into my mind. From the corner of my eye, I can see his head swivel my direction.

"And what decision might that be?" he asks, a hint of apprehension in his voice.

"I've decided I definitely want to do photography as a business. As my job."

He immediately looks both relieved and excited all at once. "That's awesome, Quinn. You're an amazing photographer." He gets up to place the kabobs on the grill but looks back at me to ensure that I know he's listening.

"Thank you. I'm not sure what exactly I'll do yet. Whether it's building my own business and doing lifestyle shoots, maybe weddings, too…or maybe I'll work for the local newspaper—I haven't figured it all out yet. I just know that I've fallen in love with it, and I want to be able to do it full-time."

He shuts the grill and returns to my side on the bench, grabbing my hand in the same movement.

"I love that you've found something you love so much— wait, you said the local newspaper? Does this mean there's a chance you'll stay here? On Oahu?" Hope and excitement dance in his dark eyes. I laugh at his adorable eagerness and let his stare send a rush of warmth through me.

"I'd say there's a decent chance," I say with a smile, placing a hand on his cheek, my thumb lightly grazing his skin. I'm hesitant to say it with absolute certainty because there's still a part of me that feels restless and antsy, but I do know that, overall, planting roots here is the most appealing option to me right now. The pull I feel toward Brian and the level of comfort we share is unlike anything I've ever felt before. The buzz of excitement that awakens in me just by being around him is stronger than any fleeting feeling or momentary adrenaline rush I've ever experienced.

We've grown especially close over the last couple weeks. After I broke down in front of him about my grief, we bonded in such a unique way. We connected on such a deep level that day that it set the tone for our relationship going forward, which has only grown stronger as time's gone on. It's kind of surreal to me, given how I've always looked at relationships, but it just feels right somehow.

He gets up to flip the kabobs and then comes back to sit down. The way he's looking back at me only makes my heart swell and confirms that what we have would be completely devastating to let go of. He leans in to brush his lips against mine, sending a shiver down my spine. I know he meant it to be a quick kiss, but I kiss him back, and I find it to be far too cautious and gentle for my liking. Goosebumps spark across the top of my skin, and my heart rate picks up when he runs his hand up the length of my arms. I'm all of a sudden desperate for more, not feeling nearly close enough. So, after a moment, I keep my mouth just an inch away from his and twist to straddle his lap on the swing, my hair cascading around his face, my lips brushing against his widening grin.

"How much longer on the food?" I murmur, moving to kiss his jawline, nerves sparking where his hands are gripping my waist. They tighten firmly, confirming that he's right there with me, feeling the same strong urge that I am.

"What food?" he answers, slipping both of his hands up

underneath the back of my tank top, running them all the way up the length of my back. I kiss him hard on the mouth, gripping the tops of his arms, which flex as he squeezes me closer to him. In one swell movement, he rises, sliding his arm underneath to hold me up. I pepper kisses down his neck while he uses one hand to set the kabobs on a clean plate, then dips us to turn off the propane tank.

We leave the food where it is, all but forgotten, as he carries me inside the house—where we don't even make it past the couch.

"Sit still, Kaikamahine (daughter)," my mother says to me as she brings a brush to my hair. I'm sitting in a chair on a Friday in front of the bathroom vanity where I'm getting ready to pick up a friend for the football game at the high school. She pulls the brush down, trailing her hand after it to smooth out my hair as she goes. I watch as her gaze follows the direction of her hand and then flicks up to my reflection in the mirror.

"What's worrying you, sweet girl?" She always had a knack for knowing when something was bothering me, even if I hadn't said it out loud.

"Stupid boy drama." I roll my eyes dramatically. She smiles knowingly with a shake of her head.

"I remember those days," she says.

"Ugh, it's so frustrating," I spit out, and she quirks an eyebrow, which prompts me to continue on. "Remember Peter? The guy that I've had a crush on for the last year? He told everyone at school today that he's taking Bridget to the school dance. He says I'm not the kind of girl he usually goes for. Apparently, I'm too much for him, and he wants someone more low-key. What does that even mean?" I cross my arms in annoyance. Mom studies me quietly for a moment.

"Quinn, listen to me." She sets the brush down and places both of her hands on my shoulders, meeting my eyes in the mirror. "Don't let anyone convince you to change who you are. If they can't see how absolutely amazing you are, then they don't deserve to know you. Period. Don't change yourself for anyone else's approval—no matter who they are. Don't give anyone else that power, okay?"

"I know. Thanks, Mom," I reply half-heartedly, soaking in her words but also knowing that she's just telling me what most moms would say to their daughters in this situation.

"I'm serious," she says with a squeeze of her hands. "You are one of a kind, sweetheart. Not too much, not too little. You're just perfect. Don't let anyone else dim your light, okay?" She dips her head to catch my wandering gaze in the mirror. "Promise?" she asks.

I smile, allowing her words to slightly overshadow Peter's. "Okay, Mom. Promise." Her face softens as I get out of the chair.

"I've gotta get going, or else I'll be late. I'll see you later, okay?" I say to her as she grabs my cell phone and hands it to me on my way out of the bathroom.

"Love you!" she calls after me.

My eyes open with a start, and I blink them a few times, a deep ache in my chest from the memory of one of the last times I was with my mom. Their accident was two nights after our little chat in my bathroom. I swipe at the tear that falls down the side of my face into Brian's pillow. I let the sadness run through me, taking deep breaths to help feel my way through it. I don't want to shove the memories down anymore. Or push thoughts of my parents away. I want to feel it all—the good and the bad. With a shaky breath, I whisper, *"aloha au iā 'oe mau loa. I love you forever."*

"Quinn?" Brian asks from behind me. Although my chest tightens at his voice, instead of panicking this time, I only feel a melancholy type of calm as I turn onto my other side to face him. I'm guessing it must be early morning, judging by the subtle light seeping in from the windows.

"You okay?" Concern deepens his brows and the crease between his eyes. I do my best to give him a small smile.

"I'm okay," I whisper, shifting closer to him until I can press my forehead to his chest, my arms curled in front of me. I slide my top leg between his, and his strong arm wraps over me, resting his hand on my back.

"Was it a dream?" he asks quietly.

"Yeah." I nod while letting out a deep sigh. "It feels different, though. It's hard to explain… The pain is still there. It hurts, and I can feel the tears prickling at the surface, but I don't have the urge to jump out of bed. That's probably a good sign, right?"

"I'd think so." He moves his fingers until they're scratching softly across my back. We sit in silence for a few minutes while I fully sink into the comfort of him, matching my breath with the rise and fall of his chest.

"Can I ask you a question?" He asks, his voice breaking slightly, either from morning grogginess or from emotion. I nod my head against his chest, breathing in the warm, woodsy scent of him.

"What was it that you whispered?" His voice is deep and slow. A lump immediately forms in my throat, but I'm able to swallow it down.

"Aloha au iā 'oe mau loa. It means *I love you forever*." I bring my head back to look up at him, resting my chin against him. "My mom always whispered those words to me at bedtime. Every single night—even when I was too old to be tucked in anymore. If she was already sleeping by the time I got home, then, she'd leave a Post-it note on my bedroom door for me to see when I went to bed."

He doesn't say anything. He doesn't need to. The tightening

of his grip around me is all I need. We lie entangled with each other in a comfortable silence, the quiet hum of our breathing the only sound filling the air until, eventually, I drift back to sleep.

31

———————

BRIAN

"I think I won," Quinn breathes heavily, collapsing onto the sand next to me, letting her surfboard land with a thud.

"No way. I got barreled into that last wave. That totally counts as double points. Maybe triple," I reply, trying to catch my own breath, "that was a sweet tail slide you did, though."

I asked Quinn this morning how she wanted to spend our time before I take her to the airport this afternoon. When she chose surfing, we walked the short steps from my house with our boards to surf for the last couple hours. I peer over at where Quinn's lying, spread out like a starfish on the beach. There's a small clump of wet sand sticking to her dark wavy hair that's splayed out haphazardly next to her head. Her eyes are closed, and the corners of her lips are pulling up into a wild grin, fully lost in the post-surfing high. It's moments like these, when she's completely present—no matter what we're doing—when she's soaking it all in, that she looks the most beautiful to me. The way her whole body lights up, radiating energy as if it's too much to hold inside.

"I'm going to miss this," she says quietly.

"Surfing?" I ask her, shaking excess water out of my hair with my hand.

"No. Well, yes. But I meant just being here with you."

I smile, grabbing her open hand that's closest to me, resting mine on top of hers.

"I'll miss you, too," I say quietly. She's not even gone yet, and I'm already dreading the next ten days. We've spent every spare second together lately, and somehow, it hasn't been nearly enough. As someone who hasn't been great at making time for relationships in the past, the way I feel about Quinn has completely changed that. Maybe it's because she's the first person who's ever made me feel this way—not just about her, but about myself, too. She makes me feel like I deserve to prioritize myself, that I'm worth doing that. That there's more to life than hustling. Everything about my life and the decisions I make has changed now that my focus has shifted. My priorities now include not only Quinn, but also myself.

"We've got an hour before we should head to the airport," I say. "Do you want to head back and get cleaned up?"

She turns her head my way and pushes her bottom lip out in a pout before rolling onto her stomach, then pushing up to stand.

"I suppose."

We gather our boards and start the walk back through the sand. Dipping under the low-hanging palm tree on the right side of my house, I lead her to the outdoor shower that's opposite the hammock. Turning the handle on, I turn to Quinn, who's smirking at me with a glint of mischief in her eyes.

"Oh," she says flirtatiously with a smile, "are we going to have a shower moment?"

I chuckle, checking the temp of the water with my right hand, my left still entangled with hers. I move to hover closer to her face for a second, just before our lips meet.

"Only if you want to," I say thickly before pressing my lips to hers in a quick peck. I gently guide her through the water stream until we're standing in the middle of the shower, both of us on opposite sides of the water stream, so it hits the sides of our bodies evenly.

I slowly run my hands up and down her arms to help the rushing water carry sand down her body and into the drain by our feet. She does the same for me, running her hands up the side of my torso, her hands leaving a trail that's slightly warmer than the water.

She steps closer to me, closing the gap between us until her stomach is gently pressed to mine. The water streams where our bodies are connected, the temperature of it only adding to the heat from our bodies. Her soft eyes have a hold over me, sucking me in, getting lost in them for a moment until I feel an almost desperate urge to blurt out what I'm feeling before we run out of time and she's gone.

"Quinn," I say quietly, tucking a piece of wet hair behind her ear, "I really want to say this to you before you leave this afternoon…and you don't have to say it back if you're not ready, but I just need you to know—"

"I love you," she blurts out, her brows flying up in surprise at her own words. I'm left speechless as I take in her words. Her face softens with conviction as she reaches out to grab my hand under the water. Emotion runs through me as I bring my other hand up to cup her cheek. Bringing my head forward, I rest my forehead against hers, our eyes locked together.

"I love you, too, Quinn," I whisper, knowing with certainty that I've never spoken truer words. She grins up at me with unbridled emotion before closing her eyes, getting lost in the moment again.

"You do?" she says softly. I nod my head, still pressed against her head, until I move to bring my lips to hers, hoping that the kiss will portray the magnitude of all the feelings running through me. How much I love her. How she's more important to me than anyone else in the world. How much I'll miss her. How much I desperately wish that she'll decide to not move away, even though I would never ask her to stay just for me.

She brings her arms up and around my neck while I rest my hands on the small of her wet back. I bring my lips to hers and press my hands into her, pulling her into me. She runs her hands down my chest, resting them against my abs while I run a hand up her back to tuck under her bikini strap. We spend a few minutes completely lost in each other, the warm water and our bodies creating a steam that swirls around us.

"We should get going," I mumble against her lips, my thumb grazing the skin of her back. "You've got a plane to catch." She nods back, the same conflicting emotions that I feel clearly written all over her face, too.

"Here." I step away from her to grab a beach towel from a hook on the far edge of the shower area. She shuts the water off, and then I slide the towel around her shoulders, wrapping her up tightly. I do the same with a towel of my own and follow her into the house to get changed.

"Is this really all you're bringing?" I gesture to her one suitcase after we're fully dressed.

"Yup," she says proudly, running her fingers through her still-wet hair, "just that one suitcase and then this bag for my carry-on. I've got my camera in here, so I can keep it with me." She smiles.

"I'm impressed." I nod my head in approval, sliding a baseball cap on and reaching for my keys on the kitchen counter.

"I'm an efficient traveler," she says as she slings the smaller bag over her shoulder. I pick up the suitcase, and we walk the path outside to my truck.

The ride to the airport is quiet as I hold her hand on top of the center console. There's not much to say, and I'm straddling a line of being excited for her and wanting her to fully embrace this trip, but I also feel dread and sadness trying to surface when I think of how lonely the next ten days are going to be.

When we get to the airport, I follow the signs to get to terminal two. After weaving through the steady stream of cars, I find an open spot by the curb to pull next to.

"You don't have to get out if you don't want to," she says, looking over at me. "I can grab my bags myself."

"You should know me better than that by now, Quinn." I give her a small smile. "Besides, you deserve a proper goodbye." I catch a small hint of pink spreading on her cheek as she smiles and opens her door.

I climb out to grab her suitcase and meet her on the other side, where she had set her carry-on bag on the ground by her feet. Without warning, she jumps into my arms as soon as I'm close enough, wrapping her arms around my neck. I smile, sliding my arms around her lower back, squeezing firmly. People pass around us, walking in and out of the airport, but my focus is only on her. She's the first to pull back, but only enough to look me in the eyes.

"I'll be back," she says pointedly, bringing her hands to rest on either side of my neck. "This isn't me running, okay? I'll be back. I want to come back."

I smile at her before giving her a kiss.

"I know," I reply softly. "Go have fun." I simply watch as she slings the bag over her shoulder and then pops the handle for the suitcase. She starts walking backward toward the entrance door, keeping her eyes on me and a smile on her face.

"I love you," I call out softly yet loud enough for her to hear. Somehow, the grin on her face gets even bigger.

"I love you, too, Brian Sanderson. See you in ten days." With that, she turns and walks through the sliding door, offering me one last smile before she disappears into the airport.

32

BRIAN

"Man, this was the highlight of our trip for sure," says the last guy from the charter group as he steps onto the dock and holds his hand out to shake mine.

"Ah, that means a lot to me," I reply, returning the handshake, then handing him a small white piece of paper. "I'm glad we were able to get some nice mahi for you guys. I wrote down a list of the local restaurants who'll be more than happy to cook it up for you."

"Awesome, thanks again!" he says with a wave before joining the rest of his group as they walk off the docks. Feeling accomplished at another successful charter trip, I get working on my post-charter checklist, starting with picking up any trash and towels thrown haphazardly around the boat and wiping down the interior. My phone dings from my pocket just as I'm about to put the cleaning solution away.

Quinn: Miss you! Meet Henry.

An image comes through just behind her text, a selfie of her standing next to an elephant, a glimpse of the vast African grassland in the backdrop. Her hair is up in a topknot, and I can see the top of her camera strap sitting above the olive-green strap of her tank top. She has her sunglasses on, and her smile is stretched from ear to ear. My chest twinges at the sight of how beautiful she looks.

Brian: Miss you more. Hi, Henry.

Quinn: Back to the safari. Call you later! Love you.

Brian: Love you.

With a smile, I take one last look at the picture, then slide my phone back into my pocket. Quinn's been gone for six days now, and as much as I miss her, I'm also really happy that she's having a good time. Although cell reception is spotty where she is, so we haven't had many voice conversations, she is able to text. I've received message after message, picture after picture, at all hours of the day, and it makes me smile every single time my phone dings.

She's shown me all of the animals that she's gotten up close and personal with, all of the new friends she's made, and almost every single African cuisine meal that she's eaten. A small part of me feels like I'm right there with her, and a bigger part of me wishes I was. Not necessarily because of where she is, but for the simple fact that I miss her like crazy.

"Yo, man," Matt calls from the dock. I look up to see him and Elliot walking toward the boat.

"What's going on, boys?" I ask, wiping at the perspiration by my hairline from standing in direct sunlight.

"Not much…we're having a boy's day. Elliot wanted to swing by and say hi. Need any help with the boat?"

"I won't turn any help down." I gladly hand Matt a towel as he steps into the boat, reaching back to help Elliot across.

"I'm almost done with the interior. If you guys wouldn't mind finishing toweling off the bow of the boat, that would be great."

They move to the front of the boat while I raise the boat higher on the lift, so it's completely out of the water, then connect the hose to the engine to flush the saltwater out of it.

"What have you been doing on your boy's day?" I ask.

"We went to the driving range this morning. He's trying to teach me how to golf," Elliot says matter-of-factly.

"Trying is right," Matt huffs. "This kid is better at golf than I am. You should see his swing."

I laugh as I climb carefully onto the dock, grabbing my deck brush and soap. Once the bucket is filled with water and soap, I dip the brush and start washing the saltwater off the exterior of the boat, just like I do every time the boat's been in the ocean, which is almost daily.

"So, when does Quinn get back?" Matt asks with a smirk, grabbing another brush to help.

"Four days," I respond instantly.

"You counting down the minutes?" he chuckles.

"Pretty much," I say confidently.

He pauses his brush strokes and looks over at me. "This thing with you guys…it's real, huh? I've never seen you with that look on your face. It's weird."

"Realest thing I've ever felt," I tell him honestly, continuing to scrub, not seeing any point in downplaying what we have. Not anymore.

"Hey, I'm happy for you, man. I thought it was just a fling, but apparently, I was wrong. Just don't screw it up. Don't make us all have to choose sides, okay?"

"Not planning on screwing anything up."

He gives a nod, resuming his work. We finish up with the soap, rinse it all down, and then towel dry as much as we can.

"We're going to meet Paige in town for lunch. You want to join us?" Matt asks as he helps Elliot climb over the side of the boat.

"Nah, I have to swing by my mom's house to check-in. I haven't been by in a while. Thanks, though." I shake his hand and ruffle Elliot's hair. "See ya later, Elliot. Call me if you need a challenge in golf and want some pointers from someone who actually has a decent drive."

Matt rolls his eyes and puts his arms around Elliot as they walk away. I can't help but laugh to myself while I finish up the last couple things on the boat, then head up the stairs to my truck.

I drive with the windows rolled down, heat from the sun beaming onto the side of my face as I drive through town. I get stuck at a crosswalk for longer than normal as streams of barely clothed people carrying towels and beach bags walk across the road to the beach. Eventually, I get past the congestion of tourists to my mom's house and knock on the door as I push it open.

"Hello?" I call out.

"Oh, we're up here, Brian!" Mom says from the kitchen. I walk up the steps to find her leaning over the counter, looking at a three-ring binder that Ethan is also hunched over and pointing at. It catches me off guard because it looks like they're actually conversing in a two-sided conversation, and Ethan is a willing participant, which is an unusual sight.

"What's up?" I ask. Mom smiles and gives me a quick hug before resuming her position.

"Ethan was just telling me about the project he's working on at school. You should see, honey. It's really great!" Her eyes light up with pride.

"What's it about?" I ask Ethan, taking a soda out of the fridge before sliding next to him in a chair.

"It's a project for my science class. We had a choice between doing a science experiment or doing an engineering project and building something. I chose to build my own DC motor using a switch motor kit and electromagnets. Turned out pretty cool." He slides the binder over to me. It's filled with pictures and details of his materials and of the process he took to build it. The last page in the binder is a picture of the final motor, and I have to admit, it's pretty impressive.

"You did this all on your own?"

"Yup," he replies, shutting the binder, "got an A."

"Ethan, that's wonderful," Mom says, clearly overwhelmed with pride.

"When did you get so invested in a school project? I thought you were too cool for school," I tease, "what with all the ladies you could be talking to instead."

"Whatever." He rolls his eyes, but there's a hint of playfulness behind them.

"I'm serious. I'm proud of you." I clap my hand on his back. "You've really stepped it up lately. And you seem to have a knack for engineering—building and fixing things. You fixed the washing machine, not to mention the generator on the boat. And you said you've been refurbishing boats, right?"

He shrugs his shoulders in an attempt to brush off the compliment, but I can see the look of accomplishment on his face.

"Yeah, I'm definitely interested in stuff like that. I guess I'm good at it, too."

"Absolutely," Mom says excitedly. I notice that Ethan's not rolling his eyes or brushing her off, which is a major improvement in comparison to how he normally interacts with her. Maybe they're finally turning a corner in their relationship. I can only hope, at least.

"How about you, sweetie?" She turns to me. "What's new with you? You still seeing that nice young lady? John's sister?"

"Quinn," I offer her name, "and yup. Things are going good. Great, actually."

She smiles warmly, grabbing my hand. "I'm glad. I'm happy you're happy, honey."

"She's out of town, but I'll bring her by when she's back. We can have dinner together or something," I offer.

"Oh, I'd love that." Her smile reaches her eyes this time, and her whole face lights up. "Speaking of meals, do you boys want to stay for lunch? I can whip up a salad and some sandwiches before my shift this afternoon."

"Sounds good to me," I reply.

"Sure." Ethan shrugs. I watch as Mom bounces around the kitchen, elation practically beaming off of her.

33

QUINN

"Eeek!" I drop my luggage and jump right into Brian's arms in the middle of the busy airport. I wrap my legs around his waist and squeeze my arms around his shoulders, burying my face into the side of his neck as swarms of people rush by us in every different direction.

His strong arms encircle me, and I breathe in the woodsy smell of his skin, not entirely sure if it's his heart I feel thumping or mine. Being on this trip felt different than any of the others. I still enjoyed myself and soaked in every second of the adventure, sure, but there was also a part of me that was restless the whole time, like that part of me wanted to be somewhere else more. I've never felt that way before on any of my travels.

"Missed you," he murmurs into my hair. I squeeze him harder, then lift my head to kiss him.

"I missed you, too." I smile at him, planting another kiss on his lips before hopping down. He grabs my luggage and my hand at the same time. We walk slowly out of the airport, not in a rush anymore, now that we found each other. It feels so good to be with him again that I can practically feel a tiny piece of my restless heart settle, like maybe this is what it wanted the whole time I was gone. Just to be near him.

"Where to?" he asks when we hop into his truck.

"Your place?" I ask hopefully. I've desperately missed his beachside bungalow. I daydreamed of it often while I was gone, of the way that it's hidden underneath picturesque palm trees with the ocean view that I love so much.

"You got it," he says with a smile, reversing his truck out of the parking lot, then grabbing for my hand, "How was the flight?"

"Long. Boring. What did I miss here while I was gone?" I ask.

"Absolutely nothing," he chuckles. "Nothing ever changes around here. You know that."

"I'm realizing that I actually love that, though," I say softly with a smile, enjoying the scenic tropical views as we drive. I pull my right foot up, crossing it to rest it on the seat, pushing it against the inside of my left thigh. It's quiet in his truck except for the quiet crooning coming from the radio, a comfortable silence falling between us.

We pull into his driveway, and I hop out to grab my bag from the backseat while Brian grabs my suitcase. As we walk along the path around the side of the house, I feel another small piece of my heart settle, like my heart missed this place just as much as it did Brian. Realization hits me that his beachside bungalow feels more like home to me than any place has in years.

I let the peace from that realization resonate deep in my bones as Brian opens the door, and we set my bags just inside. Before we get too far into the house, I wrap my arms around his middle, wrapping him in a hug.

"You know what I missed the most? Besides you?" I look up at him with a smile.

"What's that?" He smirks, bringing his hands to a clasp behind my back.

"That hammock."

His dark eyes pierce into mine as he squeezes his hands against my back. "Well, let's get you in that thing, then."

I follow him out to the hammock, where he climbs in first, widening his legs for me to settle between them, wobbling a little as I get in, resting my back against his chest, my head tucked under his chin so that we're both facing the same way. He wraps his arms around the top of my chest, and I bring my hands up to rest on top of his arms. The hammock bounces softly as my eyes catch on a bird in the distance that's flying above the ocean's waves, swooping closer to the water before retreating higher. I watch, mesmerized, as the bird repeats the cycle over and over again.

"So, what was your favorite part of your trip?" he asks softly in my ear.

"Hmm, it's so hard to choose. Honestly, probably just getting up close to all of the animals. We saw cheetahs, lions, leopards, giraffes…oh, and a hyena!"

"Did you see any rhinos?" he asks, his breath tickling the space between my ear and my hair.

"Several." I nod my head. "I'll show you the pictures once I edit them a little bit…actually, now that I think about it, that may have been my favorite part. Photographing everything. Having my camera with me added a whole new layer to the trip that I've never experienced before. It was pretty cool."

"I'm happy for you, Quinn," he murmurs, and I can feel the vibration of his voice through his chest. "Hey, what did you choose for your jewelry souvenir?"

"Oh, I got a set of cream-and-gold hand-beaded bangle

bracelets. And I brought you back a carved wooden elephant bottle opener."

"Awesome," he chuckles, squeezing me tighter, "can't wait to use it. I'm glad you had a good time."

"I did have a good time." I smile, welcoming an urge to open up to him. "But you know what? I realized something while I was gone. Do you want to hear?"

"Of course."

"So, normally, when I'm traveling, I'm usually fully immersed in it, completely focused and invested in wherever I am, right? Well, it was different this time. I couldn't get Oahu out of my head while I was there. I kept thinking about everything here that I was missing out on. Even just the day-to-day boring stuff that had me dying of boredom a year ago. I missed it. A part of me craved the mundane, slower life that's here."

"Really?" He sounds surprised and pleased at the same time.

"Yeah. I'm not saying I don't want to travel because I definitely do. But I don't want to move anywhere else. I want Oahu to be my home base." I can feel his chest expand as he takes a deep breath in, processing my words.

"You have no idea how happy that makes me, Quinn," he says quietly. I smile and squeeze where I'm holding his arm.

"Besides, I would be a very stupid woman if I moved away and left you available for someone else to scoop up."

He chuckles, gripping me just a tad bit tighter as we listen to the waves crashing onto the nearby shore.

"How are things with Ethan? And your mom?" I ask him after a little while.

"Great, actually." He sounds like he almost doesn't believe it himself. "They seem to be getting along better than they used to. I think it all stems from Ethan. I don't know if he's just maturing or discovering things that he's passionate about, but he's really come into his own lately, and he's putting more of an effort into everything—school, his relationship with Mom, even work. He's been calling me more and more on the weekends to see if he can tag along on charters, even when I don't technically need his help."

"Wow, that's great," I reply. "Good for him. Have you made any decisions about the tournament money?"

"No. Still sitting on it. I don't think another boat is the best option, though. At least not for Ethan to captain. He seems to be really interested in building and fixing things, so maybe he wants to go down a different route. I'm not sure. I'll have to have a conversation with him at some point soon. Fishing might not even be what he wants to do. I don't really know anymore."

I nod, letting the quiet take over, completely comfortable in his arms.

"I should probably get my luggage back to my apartment," I say regretfully, not wanting to ruin this perfect moment but knowing that I should probably get up, "do some laundry, check on everything. My mail is probably overflowing."

"Why don't you leave it? Your stuff?" Brian asks quietly but confidently.

"I guess I could stay 'til tomorrow," I agree with a smile.

"How about longer than that? Why don't you just stay here? Move here?"

My head pops off of his chest in shock, and after a brief moment to absorb what he said, I twist around until I'm lying on his stomach, hovering just above his face.

"Brian Sanderson. Are you asking me to move in with you?" I ask him with a smile, feeling excited and happy, surprised that there's no trace of apprehension or nerves.

"Only if you want to." He grins, his dimple deepening on his cheek, and I can't help but shake my head slowly and mirror his smile. It doesn't take me long at all to come to a decision.

"I would love to," I whisper, bringing myself forward to kiss him, my right hand holding the span of his cheek where it meets his ear. I let the emotions run through me, along with the buzz of excitement, allowing myself to revel in the contentment that I feel. When I pull away, my thumb grazes his cheek, and I get lost in his dark eyes.

"Also, I already collected your mail for you. It's in a pile on my kitchen counter," he says.

"Of course you did," I say with a smile and then return my lips to his.

34

———

BRIAN

"Here, take some leftovers," Mom says, shoving a container of grilled chicken into Quinn's hands, topping it with another container filled with chopped veggies while we stand at the doorway of her house.

"Thank you," laughs Quinn, "are you sure?"

"Absolutely. There's plenty left here for Ethan and me tomorrow. You go ahead and take it." Mom looks absolutely giddy, basking in the aftermath of the meal we just shared together. Quinn and my mom chatted all throughout dinner, falling into easy conversation and laughter while Ethan and I just watched and shrugged at each other. They've met before, obviously, but only briefly, and there's a certain air of excitement now that Quinn and I are officially living together. Mom has been absolutely ecstatic at these recent events, not even attempting to tone down her overflowing enthusiasm toward us.

"If you insist." Quinn leans over to give her a one-handed hug goodbye.

"You hang onto this one, honey," Mom whispers in my ear as she wraps her arms around me. "This one's a keeper."

"I know, Mom," I reply with a smile before turning to Ethan, who's holding his hand out for me to shake. I try not to stumble on the gesture, given the rarity of how often he's ever offered his hand.

"Can I come with you on your charter tomorrow? Five-thirty at the docks, right?" Ethan asks me earnestly.

"Sure," I tell him, returning his handshake. "I'll never turn down another set of hands. Quinn might tag along to take pictures, too."

"Cool." He nods.

I open the door and let Quinn pass by onto the sidewalk, offering one last smile to my mom before catching up with Quinn.

"That was fun," Quinn says once we're inside the truck. "I can tell how much your mom loves you and Ethan. You're really lucky to have her." She smiles genuinely.

"She's sacrificed a lot for us," I say in agreement. "Blowin' in the Wind" by Bob Dylan comes on the radio—one of my favorites—so I turn the volume up a few notches, settling into a comfortable drive back. I pass by the road that leads to my house, instead turning right toward a stretch of beach where several food trucks are arranged along the parking lot next to where the sand begins.

"What are we doing?" Quinn asks with a sly grin.

"I thought I'd take you to get a malasada puff before heading home to finish unpacking," I say, making her eyes light up as wide as saucers.

"Oh, I love everything about that sentence," she says dreamily.

"Figured you would," I laugh, climbing out of the truck. We

walk hand in hand to the yellow-and-white-striped bakery food truck to get in line behind a gentleman with a straw hat and a cringe-able sunburn line that sits just above his swim trunks.

"Do you know what flavor you want?" I ask, peering around the man to scan the menu that lists all of the custard filling options for the inside of the fried doughnut.

"That's such a hard choice," Quinn muses, tapping her finger against her bottom lip, "but I think I'll go with guava."

When it's our turn, I pay for our puffs—guava for her, chocolate for me. Holding the wax-paper-wrapped pastry in one hand, I follow Quinn onto the beach, where she finds an open section to sit down. She crosses her legs while I sit next to her, leaning my arms over my bent knees, sinking comfortably into the sand. We eat the puffs and people-watch the many tourists as they walk by in front of us along the water's edge.

My mind drifts to Quinn and how far we've come in our relationship the past couple months. How she went from being my best friend's little sister and childhood friend to the very center of my world. How our relationship gradually developed and deepened into something so real and profound, an emotional connection underneath it all that feels so genuine. So intentional and fated, like maybe we were always meant to be together this way.

"What do you think your parents would think of you being with me?" I wonder out loud. She turns her head to me in surprise at the random topic, but overall, she seems comfortable with the subject, just like every other time we've talked about her parents lately.

"Hmm," she muses, crumpling her leftover wrapper into a tiny ball. "I think they would have loved you." She peers at me from the corner of her eye and smiles. "Honestly, I think they would love anyone who makes me as happy as you do…but I also know they thought you were a great friend to John…so I think they'd approve of you, specifically, too."

I reach across and use my thumb to wipe a small speck of guava custard that's smeared by the corner of her mouth.

"I'm glad you think so," I say, looking back down at the sand. "I loved your parents."

She scoots closer, wrapping her arms around my arm that's resting on my knee. After a few more minutes, the sun begins its slow descent above the horizon.

"You ready to head back?" I ask. She lifts up to plant a kiss on my cheek.

"Yes," she mutters against my skin. "Race you!" She bolts up and starts running, already halfway off the beach before I'm even to my feet.

"Hey!" I yell, sprinting until I catch up to her and can wrap my arms around her waist, lifting her up, slightly stumbling on my feet. We laugh as we steady ourselves, eventually grabbing each other's hands as we walk the rest of the way off the beach. The rest of the ride back is quiet and comfortable as we weave through the familiar palm-tree-lined streets.

"After you," I say as I open the passenger-side door of my truck for her to get out when we arrive.

"Thank you, sir." The sun finishes its descent, and darkness falls as we make our way inside the house. As I shut the door behind her, I notice how different my house already feels since she moved in. To the eye, it looks mostly the same, with a few obvious additional touches here and there of her, but it's the energy in the house that feels different. Charged somehow. Quinn does everything passionately in life, and loving me is no different. She's sparked every single aspect of my life that I didn't even realize was dull, including my house. It feels lit up from the inside out from the energy she brings just by existing here.

"So, we only have these two boxes left, right?" I ask, pointing to the last stack of boxes next to the coffee table.

"Yup!" she says cheerfully. "One is marked clothes, and the other is kitchen."

"Right on. You really didn't have a lot of stuff," I ponder. "You're sure there isn't anything else left at the apartment?"

"Nope. I double-checked," she says with a shrug. "I guess I just don't have a lot of things."

I pull open the box labeled kitchen, and we continue our unpacking routine that we've ironed out the last couple days. I take the items out, remove the bubble wrap, then pass it to Quinn, who finds a new home for it.

"Espresso maker," I announce before passing it to her.

"A necessity," she comments, marching it directly to the kitchen, where she sets it next to my coffee maker.

"Coasters?" I examine the cylinder-shaped container, peeling a tiny strip of tape off of the bottom.

"Oh, those are from Dubai! Should we put them on the end table by the couch?" She sets them next to the lamp.

"Sure," I say with a shrug. The truth is, I don't really care where everything goes. As much as I loved having order and organization for every little detail of my house before, now I'm finding that it just doesn't matter. I've been loving every part of her moving in—of melding her world with mine, even if it ends up getting a little messy.

"Blender?" I hand the small appliance to her, crumpling the bubble wrap and setting it to the side.

"Oh yeah. You don't have one, right? We definitely need one for all of the killer pineapple coladas I'm planning to whip up."

I laugh, breaking down the empty box and bringing it to the front door so I can take it out to the recycling bin later.

"Clothes next?" I ask, pointing to the last box.

"Sure." She beams at me. I lift the remaining box and follow her down the hall to our bedroom.

35

QUINN

"You ready for today?" Brian asks from behind me in the kitchen, resting his left hand on my left hip while nuzzling close to plant a kiss on my right temple. Nerves buzz along the surface of my skin in anticipation, so I take yet another attempt at a deep breath to calm them.

"I think so," I say softly. I twist around until we're face to face, and I'm able to wrap my arms around his waist, pressing my cheek to his chest. My eyes catch on the bouquet of hibiscus flowers on the island that Brian brought home this morning. Yellow—my mom's favorite.

"I think it'll be nice, actually," I murmur into his shirt. He brings his arms up my back, softly scratching the tips of his fingers on the skin in between the straps of my black sundress.

"I think so, too," he says. "Should we go?"

I nod, trying to swallow down a rush of nausea. Brian grabs

the flowers in one hand, threading the fingers of his other hand with mine, and we head out the front door.

The drive is quiet, Brian giving me space to just be, grounding me to reality with the occasional squeeze of his hand. When we pull into the parking lot of the Hawaiian Memorial Park Cemetery, I muster any last ounce of strength that's inside and step out.

We walk through the beautiful lush park with vast mountains in the backdrop, passing by memorial benches and stunning cremation gardens. Varying shades of pink and purple flowers cover the rows of bushes that line the walkway. I marvel at the beauty of it all. It really is a serene and stunningly beautiful place for people to come to honor the souls of those resting here.

I spot John and Mia already standing by Mom and Dad's gravesite up ahead. Tightening my grip on Brian's hand, we quietly walk over to join them.

"Hey," I say softly in greeting as Mia gently wraps her arms around me in a hug. I let go of Brian's hand to give John a hug and then step to the side as he and Brian shake hands. We fall into place in a semi-circle, letting silence fall over us.

"Is this your first time back?" John asks quietly. He doesn't address me by name, but we all know his question is directed at me.

"Yeah." I nod. "Since the funeral." John's eyes widen, and guilt flashes across his face.

"Seriously?" he asks in shock, running his fingers through his hair. "Man, Quinn… I should have checked in with you more. Should have offered to bring you here, or whatever you needed. I feel like I really let you down."

I shake my head and angle it to make sure he's looking into my eyes.

"It's okay, John," I say quietly, grabbing his arm. "I wasn't ready."

After he nods solemnly, I move forward and crouch down,

running my fingers across Mom's headstone, tracing the outline of her name, allowing the emotions to come. A single tear falls down my cheek as Brian comes to a crouch on my left side, placing a reassuring hand on my bent leg. John lowers on my right side, and I can feel Mia's hand on the middle of my back.

Feeling grateful for their support, I give my best smile and let the tears fall as I run my hand over Dad's headstone in the same way. Closing my eyes, I let the sadness resonate right in the center of my being, deep in my soul.

We sit like that for several minutes until the sadness I'm feeling eventually becomes overpowered by a sense of peace. I take another couple of minutes to bask in the comfort of that feeling, in the quiet, and then I wipe under my eyes as I slowly stand and clear my throat.

"Thanks for coming with me, guys," I say, pushing the words through when my voice cracks.

"Of course," Mia whispers with a gentle smile.

"Thanks for inviting us," John says gruffly, sincerity behind his eyes.

Brian bends to place the yellow flowers by Mom's name, then grabs my hand as we start a slow walk back to the parking lot. After hugging John and Mia goodbye, I turn to Brian and wrap my arms around him in a hug as we stand next to his truck, drawing some much-needed strength from his embrace before climbing in. As he backs out of the lot and heads home, he stays quiet, ready to follow my lead with conversation.

I grip the top of his forearm and give a reassuring smile when his eyes connect with mine. As sad as it was to visit them, I don't feel like I'm going to drown in my grief, and it's not lost on me how big of a deal that is in and of itself. Even just a few short months ago, I couldn't even talk about them out loud. I realize how grateful I am for my relationship with Brian because, through all of it, he helped me realize so much about myself. He pointed out my inner strength and how to be proud of myself for it. He's encouraged me to go after my dreams and follow my heart. He taught me that it's okay to settle down and to feel whatever emotions I'm feeling, to not run from them.

But more than that, he helped me realize that grief doesn't have to be this all-consuming, isolating hole that I fall into every so often. Nothing will ever take away the pain from missing my parents, of course, but in his own way, Brian has shown me how to let them out of the deepest part of my heart and how to live life with them on a daily basis. To honor them in small ways and big ways, to speak the memories out loud and acknowledge them. To share them with him and others who loved my parents, too. It all feels just a little less heavy that way.

As we drive along, each deep breath seems to breathe new life into me until I feel a calmness mixing in with the peace. When we get close to our house, my brows burrow in confusion when I see several familiar cars parked along the side of the driveway.

"What's going on?" I ask with hesitation. Brian just shrugs and smiles, shifting his truck into park. When I climb out, he's already at the back of the truck, offering a hand. I eye him suspiciously as we walk around the side of the house.

The first person to come into view is Tori, who stumbles trying to catch a frisbee, falling headfirst into the sand. At further glance, I see that Elliot is the one who threw the frisbee, and Matt's giving him a high five. Paige and Noelle are sitting on a blanket closer to the shoreline.

"How'd you beat us?" John's voice comes from behind me. I spin around to see him and Mia walking around us, carrying a cooler and grocery bag onto the beach, not bothering to wait for a response. I turn my head slowly to Brian, who's smiling.

"Thought it would be a nice afternoon for a picnic," he says innocently. "Come on." Gratitude rushes through me because, somehow, Brian knew that on these days when the grief is more front and center, I might need people around me. Not necessarily as a distraction anymore, like I once needed, but more so for comfort. To remind me of all the love that I still have and that still surrounds me.

"Hey, girl!" Tori calls as I shuffle through the sand toward her. "Go long!"

I grin and run past her, looking back just in time to grip the frisbee as it comes whizzing by my side.

"Nice!" Matt calls, and I laugh, sending it over to him.

"I think we need a football rematch!" John yells, tossing it into the air.

"Oh yeah! Bring it on," says Paige, passing Noelle into Mia's eager arms.

As the afternoon goes on, my heart swells with happiness with each pass of the football, each squeal of laughter from being tackled, and every cheer of victory. These are my people, every single one of them, and I soak in the time together.

When the last hug goodbye is given, and they're all gone, Brian and I pick up every last beach toy and race back to the picturesque beachside bungalow that we call ours. The place I call home.

EPILOGUE

QUINN

One year later

"Are you trying to make my heart burst from happiness, Brian Sanderson?" I huff as he leads me up the trail next to our house.

"Nope," he laughs, his voice thickened with the same steady confidence that he's had all day. Ever since I got back from my work trip two days ago, he's been showering me with more affection than normal—which is saying a lot, given he's naturally a pretty touchy-feely guy.

Six months ago, I started working as a freelance travel photographer. I travel to different destinations around the world to take pictures for my clients, most of which are hotels and travel-related websites that then use the images for marketing material. Every once in a while, Brian's even able to free up his schedule and come with me.

I absolutely love my job. I love both the traveling aspect and the actual art of photography. It fills my heart and recharges my soul every single time I go on assignment and get to create beautiful images. And still, nothing will ever top the feeling I get when I come home to Brian and our life here. When I get home, we usually spend a few days holed up in the bungalow, not separating from each other for a single moment.

This time has been no different, except today, he's insisted on getting out of the house. We've been on a non-stop adventure from the moment we woke up. He took me to get malasada puffs to eat for breakfast on the beach while we watched the sunrise. Then, we went on a bicycle ride down the coast, followed by paddle boarding around the bay in town. Now, he's insisting on hiking the trail by the house that we walk nearly every day that leads to our favorite spot: the cliff overlook with the killer view and the sometimes-perfect diving spot—if the conditions are safe enough, of course.

"Watch your step," he says, pointing out a rock jutting into the path. We make it to the clearing at the top and walk to the edge, taking in the expansive cliff that's ahead and to the left and the rolling waves of the ocean that are crashing onto the rock below.

Off to the right, we can see the bay on the property that's bustling with movement. A forklift drives past the large excavator that's scooping away at piles of dirt. A bobcat and crane are settled on the other side of the bay, each doing their own job to make progress on the project while the construction workers bustle and move around between them.

Brian decided to use his tournament money to develop his own marina on this part of the property. This will be the main marina that he'll run his charter company from, but it's also big enough in size for plenty of other boats and businesses to dock here as well. Ethan jumped on board with the idea right away, and now that he's graduated, he plans to run the service part of the marina, overseeing the maintenance, repair, and upkeep of the boats. I'm proud of Brian and excited to watch his business expand in a way that serves not only himself but others as well, in true Brian fashion.

"This view never gets old," I sigh, once again counting my blessings that this tropical paradise is where I call home. Wrapping my arms around Brian's waist, I shake my head in amusement. "What a day—you sure know the way to my heart."

"I hope I do," he says gruffly with a squeeze before disentangling himself from me and slowly dropping to one knee, his dark eyes holding mine the whole way. I watch as it seems to happen in slow motion, goosebumps traveling the length of my entire body. He pulls a ring box out of his pocket and opens it up to me, my brain slow to process what's actually happening.

"Quinn Byrd," he starts slowly, and I gasp, covering my mouth with my hand, a shiver running down my spine with shock and excitement. "I love you with every single part of me." He clears his throat as if to steady his emotions.

"If you'll have me, I promise to always be there to support you and encourage you to chase your dreams. I promise to live a life of adventure with you. To lift you up and watch you fly, but then be your steady rock when you need a safe place to land."

I wipe a tear from my face as I let out a strangled laugh, completely overcome with emotion.

"I promise to always be your home base. To be your biggest supporter. You've added so much love and happiness to my life, and I would love nothing more than to try and do the same for you for the rest of your life. So, Quinn…" His dimple deepens as he smiles. "Will you marry me?"

I can hardly contain my excitement as my heart swells in an almost overwhelming way with the love I feel for him. I nod my head, my hand still covering my mouth.

"Of course!" I manage to squeak out, dropping to my knees to wrap my arms around him, burying my face in his neck. He brings his strong arms around me, and we hold each other, completely lost in the moment. I lean back to bring both of my hands to his cheeks, then lean in to kiss him gently.

"Yeah?" he asks, as if he needs confirmation. I rest my forehead on his and nod.

"Yeah," I whisper, sliding my hands through his hair and down the back of his neck. He kisses me again before we push up to stand. He takes the solitaire diamond with a gold band out of the ring box and slides it on my left hand.

"It's stunning, Brian," I breathe out, admiring how my hand looks with the ring on it.

"It suits you," he says as he kisses my forehead, hand on the back of my head. The next few minutes are spent reveling in the overwhelming excitement that I get to spend the rest of my life with him and imagining what that looks like. Because falling in love with him has been greater than any adventure I've ever been on—hands down.

"Should we take a picture?" he asks, pulling out his phone to take a selfie. He holds the camera up, and I squeeze in the frame, holding up my hand to show the ring, both Brian and me grinning, with the cliff and ocean in the background.

"Ah, I can't believe it." I wouldn't be able to shake the grin off my face even if I wanted to. "Let's send it to your mom," I suggest. "Tell her the news!"

"Go for it." He smiles, handing me his phone. "She already knew it was happening, but she'll be thrilled that you said yes."

I send the picture to his mom and Ethan and then pull up our latest group text with our friends.

"Friends, too?"

"Yeah," he agrees. "John knows—I asked his permission last week." I stop, lowering the phone to lock my eyes with him, unable to say anything.

Eventually, I force out a whisper, "What did I ever do to deserve you?"

He smiles softly, wrapping one arm around my shoulder as I

finish sending the picture. We stand side by side, arms wrapped around each other, looking out at the ocean as, one by one, his phone buzzes with responses from our loved ones.

Brian's mom sends every possible variation of a heart emoji, and Ethan replies with a thumbs up. John and Mia send a video of them jumping up and down in excitement, Mia's growing pregnant belly on display. Paige, Matt, and Tori all send an explosion of emojis and gifs in an outpouring of excitement and support. Brian slides his phone back into his pocket and pulls a small black bag out.

"I got you something else," he says softly.

"You did not." My eyes fly up to his. "Brian, this is more than enough."

"I know," he chuckles, "but open it." He hands the bag to me, and I reluctantly take it, opening it to pull out a beautiful, beaded bracelet with a silver plaque in the middle.

"It's beautiful," I tell him, turning it over, pausing when I see what's engraved on the underside of the plaque. Tears well in my eyes, and my hand comes up to cover my mouth again.

"I wanted to have another piece of jewelry that I could engrave to give to you today as well. Mostly as a way to honor your parents and include them in this moment." I choke out a sob, leaning into Brian's embrace.

"But also because of what it says. To remind you of them and how much they love you. And also to remind you of me because I also mean every single word, Quinn—with my whole heart."

I move to stand in front of him, so I can wrap both arms around his neck. I squeeze him tight, feeling overwhelmed with love as I lift the bracelet up in my hand to re-read the inscription.

"aloha au iā 'oe mau loa.
I love you forever."

THE END

ALSO BY MEGAN REINKING

The Hawaiian Getaway Series

The Ohana Cottage

The Summer Break

The Perfect Tide

ACKNOWLEDGMENTS

First and foremost, thank you to my husband, Nick, for your continued support and encouragement! Thank you, also, for being my sounding board, brainstorming buddy and my very own personal google when it came to the many questions I had about fishing in this book! I love you and am grateful for you.

To my kids, thank you for your excitement and for thinking that writing books is the coolest job in the world—I totally agree.

Thank you to all of my family and friends for the many ways you support and encourage me. It does not go unnoticed and I appreciate every single one of you!

To Jamie, thank you for literally being one of my biggest cheerleaders. Your words of encouragement, feedback and excitement is the reason this book was ever finished in the first place. Thank you for alpha-reading this with me, and for knowing my characters just as well (if not more) than I do.

Lindsey, your feedback and comments on this story meant the absolute world to me and were hugely helpful in the writing process! Thank you for always being available and for letting me ask you a million questions! I'm so lucky to have you as a friend and alpha/beta reader!

To my beta-readers—Erin, Carissa, and Shelby, I can't thank you enough for your thoughtful and honest critique, your love for these characters, and for sharing your excitement for this book! It means so much to me!

Thank you to my editor, Jenn Lockwood. You are amazing

and so appreciated! To my cover designer, proofreader, and everyone else who had a hand in creating this book—thank you!

Lastly, to all of the readers, book bloggers, Bookstagrammers and BookTokers, I cannot express how much your support means to me. I am so appreciative of every single comment, review, share, etc. I write these books for me, but I publish them for you. Having readers connect with my words and my stories will forever be my favorite part of this whole author thing.

ABOUT THE AUTHOR

Megan Reinking is a wife and mother who lives in Minnesota, where she spends her days reading, writing or chauffeuring her three children around town. She's a homebody who loves quiet, lazy days and connecting with family and friends.

www.ingramcontent.com/pod-product-compliance
Lightning Source LLC
Chambersburg PA
CBHW061250310726
48971CB00007B/2302